I0716343

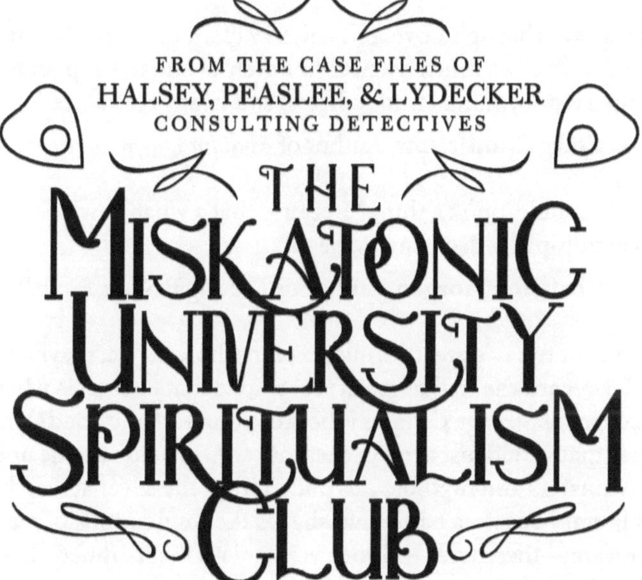

FROM THE CASE FILES OF
HALSEY, PEASLEE, & LYDECKER
CONSULTING DETECTIVES

THE
MISKATONIC
UNIVERSITY
SPIRITUALISM
CLUB

Praise for *The Miskatonic University Spiritualism Club*

"Imagine Nick and Norah Charles [from the *Thin Man* films] up against cosmic horror, Lovecraftian lore, and traditional Christmas ghost stories, and you're not far off from Peter Rawlik's charming, funny, frightening, and moving *Miskatonic University Spiritualism Club*. Save this one for bedtime on Christmas Eve—you won't regret it."

—**Shaun Hamill**, Author of *Cosmology of Monsters*

Praise for Pete Rawlik

"The coolest, most gifted Lovecraftian writer working today."

—**W. H. Pugmire**, Author of *Witches in Dreamland*

"Rawlik rampages through Lovecraft country like a grave-robber on formaldehyde. . . not so much a writer to watch as one to keep under constant supervision, animal tranquilizers, and heavy restraints."

—**Cody Goodfellow**, Author of *Radiant Dawn*, on *Reanimators*

"Is Lovecraftian pulp-punk a thing? Because that's what Rawlik's doing here, at its action-packed, cinematic best!"

—**Christine Morgan**, Author of *The Night Silver River Run Red*

"Rawlik is one of today's great conjurors of mythos, magic, mayhem and monsters. Disregard the trail of green foul smoke that emanates when you open the covers of *Strange Company*, because buried (unburied?) inside are creatures that would just as soon cheat at cards as detonate the universe into dust. Monsters and mythologies pulled from the silver screen blend with great literary beasts, a battle that shakes the foundations of reality. Readers beware—these tales will suck you in with razor-tipped claws and fling you carelessly into the void."

—**Philip Fracassi**, Author of *Behold the Void*

"Pete Rawlik is one of the most prolific and talented Lovecraftian writers put there. His work is a joy to read."

—**Mike Davis**, *The Lovecraft e-Zine*

"Rawlik's *The Peaslee Papers* transcends mere Lovecraftian homage into an area all its own, spanning time and space, slipstreaming historical characters into the mix while diving deep into occult conspiracies that linger on the mind long after the last page is turned."

—**Bob Pastorella**, *This is Horror*

Praise for *Reanimatrix*

"Rawlik takes the epistolary form through turns alternately weird, witty, and sexy in this tale of abomination and obsession, giving readers a lively romp through Lovecraft country that will leave fans of the genre hungry for more. Even better, Megan Halsey-Griffith is the anti-heroine you don't want to just read about—you want to be."

— **Wendy N. Wagner**,
Author of *The Deer Kings*

"Creating original work that pays homage to the classics without sliding into slavish imitation is a tightrope act, and one that Pete Rawlik pulls off with aplomb in *Reanimatrix*. The result is a richly inventive, Wold Newton-ish world in which Lovecraft's creations rub shoulders with figures from history, fiction, and beyond. It's a place where Dr. Jekyll, Dr. Moreau, and *My Fair Lady*'s Professor Henry Higgins can collaborate to study the 'Color Out of Space,' and really, what more could you ask for?"

— **Orrin Grey**, Author of
Guignol & Other Sardonic Tales

"Rawlik takes readers on a kaleidoscopic terror ride . . . Lovecraft connoisseurs will find much to love in this frequently gruesome and, at times, quite racy tale."

— ***Publishers Weekly***

"Blew even my vague early expectations away . . . It's fun, it's sly, it's clever. I was reminded of *The League of Extraordinary Gentlemen*."

— ***The Horror Fiction Review***

"*Reanimatrix* is a genre-blending thrill ride. . . Rawlik does a wonderful job of grabbing you and immersing you into his world. It's a true pleasure to read."

— ***The Qwillery***

"It is safe to say that at this point, Pete Rawlik knows the world of Lovecraft better than Lovecraft himself . . . *Reanimatrix* takes Lovecraft and places him squarely in the world of Raymond Chandler and Dashiell Hammett . . . It is Rawlik's most mature work to date, alternately gory and salacious but still letting the story set the pace."

— **David Goudsward**,
In a review for *Hellnotes*

Also by Peter Rawlik

NOVELS

Reanimators

*The Weird Company: The Secret History of
H. P. Lovecraft's Twentieth Century*

Reanimatrix

*The Peaslee Papers:
A Lovecraftian Chronicle*

The Eldritch Equations

COLLECTIONS

Strange Company & Others

AS EDITOR

Legacy of the Reanimator (with Brian Sammons)
The Chromatic Court

Also from Jackanapes Press

AVAILABLE NOW

Past the Glad and Sunlit Season: Poems for Halloween
by K. A. Opperman / Illustrated by Dan Sauer

October Ghosts and Autumn Dreams: More Poems for Halloween
by K. A. Opperman / Illustrated by Dan Sauer

The Withering: Poems of Supernatural Horror
by Ashley Dioses / Illustrated by Mutartis Boswell

The Voice of the Burning House
by John Shirley / Illustrated by Dan Sauer

The Ettinfell of Beacon Hill: Gothic Tales of Boston
by Adam Bolivar / Illustrated by Dan Sauer

Book of Shadows: Grim Tales and Gothic Fancies
by Manuel Arenas

The Eldritch Equations
by Peter Rawlik

Really, Really, Really, Really Weird Stories
(A New Edition with Four New Stories) by John Shirley

I Awaken in October: Poems of Halloween and Folk Horror
by Scott J. Couturier

Halloween Hearts
by Adele Gardner

Darker Than Weird: Fourteen Tales of Horror
by John R. Fultz

A Wheel of Ravens
by Adam Bolivar

Darkest Days and Haunted Ways
by Ashley Dioses

COMING IN 2024

The Exile and Other Tales of Carcosa
by Galad Elflandsson

The Black Wolf
by Galad Elflandsson

www.JackanapesPress.com
www.facebook.com/Jackanapes-Press

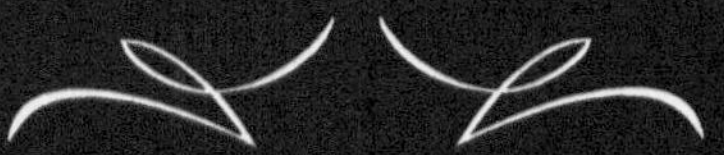

FROM THE CASE FILES OF
HALSEY, PEASLEE, & LYDECKER
CONSULTING DETECTIVES

THE MISKATONIC UNIVERSITY SPIRITUALISM CLUB

PETER RAWLIK

ILLUSTRATED BY
DAN SAUER

First Paperback Edition
3 5 7 9 8 6 4 2

ISBN: 978-1-956702-03-3

*For Gwen and Brian, who
gave me the idea.*

FROM
THE CASE FILES
OF
HALSEY, PEASLEE, & LYDECKER

CONSULTING
DETECTIVES

December 17, 1928

Two months in, and we had learned the hard way that Mondays were the worst. It seemed that horrible things happened or at least culminated on the weekends, and people sought out help first thing Monday morning. The most common of complaints were philandering spouses, an ailment that we were not inclined to associate ourselves with. Missing relatives were not exactly forbidden, but they had to have other factors that made them suited for our specific talents. The same could be said of kidnappings and murders. It's not that we weren't sympathetic, but without that taint of the outré we simply weren't interested. We did our best to direct these poor souls to the proper authorities or to private individuals that were more than capable of handling these rather mundane cases. In contrast, we kept the more interesting cases for ourselves. And paid the price.

It was mid-December, and we were licking our wounds after a particularly nasty case at the Miskatonic Club. I had taken a bullet to the shoulder, and Megan had broken three fingers on her left hand. Neither of us were in a condition to take on new work, and we should have kept the office closed, but the appointment for a consultation had been made the prior week, and it was with a member of the University faculty. As we were contracted to work with the University on security issues, we couldn't exactly cancel the meeting.

Doctor Socrates Zorba was a rather imposing figure of a man. He easily stood over six feet, but the bushy head of black hair made him look even taller. His eyes were dark beneath unkempt eyebrows and above a long aquiline nose. His mouth was lost within the mustache and beard that matched his hair both in color and wildness. His shoulders were broad, and he sat in a confident manner. His suit was well-cut, if several years out of style. There were patches on both elbows, and hints of chalk dust at the cuffs.

We were sitting in our consulting room; it was just Megan and myself as—until we knew what the situation was—we felt there was no need to involve Lydecker, our so-called senior partner. Zorba declined coffee and got right to the issue at hand. His voice was rich and clear, not quite booming, but rather a practiced tone modulated to make sure everyone could hear what he had to say. After his opening statement Megan and I exchanged glances and I asked him to repeat himself.

He seemed mildly amused. "The job is simple: I would like the two of you to join me for a ghost hunt." He noticed my lack of enthusiasm and possibly a touch of skepticism and offered an explanation. "I teach psychology at the University, and, thanks to my son Plato, function as the faculty advisor to the Miskatonic University Spiritualism Club. It's for students interested in the phenomenon of communication with the dead."

Megan made a knowing glance in my direction. "Go on," she urged him.

Zorba suddenly looked apologetic. "It's mostly just for laughs—kids scaring themselves holding séances and playing with talking boards. They've even had some mediums come down and lecture about the spirit world and ethereal bodies. From a purely psychological perspective it's fascinating stuff, almost textbook studies of delusion and the bandwagon effect. It's also given me an opportunity to document what I think of as a self-enforcing pattern of escalating fear. It seems, people like to be scared— at least a little bit—but the emotion can get out of hand, a feedback loop can develop, and this can shift fear over to absolute terror, with significant consequences."

"Are you experimenting on your students, Doctor Zorba?"

Zorba dismissed the question with a shake of his head, his wild mane swaying impressively in time with the motion. "Not at all, but I have been privileged to witness and record them experimenting on each other. I've also been forced to put a stop to things on more than one occasion. Which is why I would like you to accompany the club and me on our latest endeavor."

"Which is?" I had to admit I was curious.

"The club had wanted to investigate the Witch House, but the building inspector has declared the place unsafe. Instead we've decided to spend a week at The Krag, a fantastical piece of architecture overlooking the cove at Singing Sands. It's been abandoned since the owner Jackson Flux died back in 1922. Flux had been a Professor of Astronomy at the University until he retired in 1921. He left the estate to the University; unsurprisingly, facilities haven't a clue what to do with it. There was a thought that it could be used as a faculty retirement home, but of course it was found to be unsuitable for that purpose."

"Why is that?" Megan was obviously hooked and pushing for the rest of the story.

"I would have thought that obvious, Miss. The place is haunted. Why else would we be spending the week?"

"Haunted? How, exactly?" I was intrigued.

"Flux lost his son in an explosion in Tewksbury in 1903, and in his grief began researching the idea of communicating with the dead. He was obsessed with the idea, and in 1920 was reprimanded by the department for misappropriation of equipment, mostly radio antennas and transmitters. He claimed he had achieved communication with a ghost and had even theorized a way to capture one." Zorba rolled his eyes. "Nonsense, of course. The University let him retire in 1921. He didn't last a year before he vanished. Flux named the University as his sole beneficiary, and although he wasn't technically dead, they still felt some responsibility for the property. They hired a man, Dudley, to act as caretaker. Over the years Dudley has sent several letters detailing strange occurrences at the house, mostly weird noises and strange shadows—nothing tangible, really, but Dudley won't stay in the house after dark. The University has pretty much ignored the whole situation."

"Until now," mumbled Megan.

"Until now," shot back Zorba. "It's been seven years, Flux has been declared legally dead. If we can clear up The Krag's reputation, debunk Dudley's claims, I could convince the University to let me use it as a place for people with nervous afflictions to recuperate."

"An asylum, like Sefton?" There was a hint of condemnation in Megan's voice.

"A place of rest, where people can be healed and taught to cope with their failings and become part of society again."

My intrigue was wearing thin. "And you want us to do what, exactly?"

"I don't want you to do anything. If it was up to me, I would drive the kids down, we would spend a few nights, and then leave. However, the death of Walter Gilman and the Dunwich Horror still weigh heavily on the minds of the administration. They would like—they *require*—someone to act as security for excursions such as this, to protect the students."

"From what, exactly—ghosts?" My intrigue had turned into annoyance.

"In my experience, Mr. Peaslee, there are no such things as ghosts, and I don't expect to experience anything over the holidays to change my mind. No, at best you will be there to protect the club from something else entirely."

Megan leaned forward in piqued interest. "What would that be?"

Zorba leaned back in his chair and smiled a malignant smile, "Why, the most insidious monsters to ever exist, Miss Halsey—the students themselves." Megan looked at me. We both knew better. We both knew we shouldn't get involved. We both knew this wasn't going to end well. But then we both turned to Zorba and asked the same question. "When do we leave?"

December 24, 1928
– Morning –

It took us three hours to drive from Arkham to the house called The Krag. Megan and I followed the directions given to us by Zorba; taking a road that ran along the Miskatonic River, and turning north before the land began to rise into Kingsport Head. Driving on, we skirted Martin's Beach and then crawled through the sleepy town of Manchester. Much is said of the rising wild hills of western Massachusetts, but few have commented on the winding roads of the coast. The uneven coastline undulates between low plains, and sandy hills and rock-lined cliffs and all along this the roads twist and turn like a blind, writhing serpent trying to catch particularly elusive prey. The boulders do not help, nor do the well-concealed farm roads and crossroads, nor do the randomly placed and frequently unmarked blind intersections. There is an opinion that drivers in Massachusetts are the worst in the country, incurring more accidents than any other state in the union. I attest that this statistic is highly plausible—though the cause is not the poor skills of the state's drivers, but rather the deplorable condition of its roads and associated signage. These roads were an extension of New England's deeply bred stoicism, for I watched astounded as they matter-of-factly navigated these treacherous curves at speeds even I found uncomfortable. More than once, I was surprised by a truck or car pulling out from a blind driveway into our path and forcing me to perform increasingly desperate evasive maneuvers.

North of Manchester we turned east, following a private road that was little more than a wide trail of crushed shells. The tall grass on either side slowly gave way to scraggly dune grass and sea oats. There were trees, tall windswept things that swayed in the breeze. These hid the coastline, but I could hear the waves crashing on the rocky beach below. Then we took a turn and found the gates and fence that marked the boundary of the property. The lower portion was a rather common short wall made from what I assumed was local stone. Out of this, at a regular interval of two feet, jutted black iron rods about an inch in diameter. Most of these rose into the air about eight feet and ended in a stylized fleur-de-lis, but every sixth one shot half as high again. Two horizontal bands of metal ran through all of them, binding them to each other. The gates were made of the same material supported by two massive iron pillars. Above the gates the ironwork seemed to take on more of an artistry. The simple lines took on more angles and began to weave through each other, forming a number of shapes that reminded me vaguely of the decorations found amongst the Pennsylvania Dutch. As we passed under them, I saw that the decorated arch was much thicker than the bands running through the fence. It would have to be, I supposed, just to support itself. Once inside the gates we passed into a thick copse of ancient oaks—even in winter the dead leaves blocked the sun—and for a brief moment we were all plunged into darkness, and then the road turned, and I saw The Krag for the first time.

It squatted on the cliff side, a long-forgotten ruin forged by architects with an idealized concept of what New England architecture should look like, rather what New England architecture actually looked like. There was a great variation in the type and quality of stone and wood used, giving the impression that the house had been built not all at once, but rather in pieces, and over decades. The ground level of the three-story edifice consisted of massive stonework, on top of which a semicircular-shaped shingle-sided structure had been layered. The main house sported a gambrel roof as well as a large porch that jutted out toward the ocean. A tower capped with a dome rose up from behind the house and melded into the supporting stonework. I counted at least three chimneys rising up out of the mansion like pillars pointing the way to heaven. Through the arch I could see the cliff and beyond that the sea, a distant rolling ocean of slate waters that stretched out to the horizon, reflecting back the grey clouds that had gathered along the coast.

Out of the car, as I stretched my legs, it seemed to me that we were intruding in this place, disturbing it. I couldn't help but think of the house as a living thing that had long slumbered undisturbed and contented, like a cat basking in the morning sun. And now we were here, a noisome coterie of mice making ourselves busy, blissfully unaware of the danger we risked in rousing the giant.

"Someone has been here recently," remarked Megan as she opened the trunk.

"Hmm?" I asked as I joined her. We started unloading our equipment. She made a hand gesture. "The lawn was cut before winter set in, and the bushes have been trimmed back. The flowerbeds have been weeded. There's a cord of fresh firewood at the end of the drive."

I nodded, taking in the grounds and the details that Megan noted. "Zorba said there was a caretaker—Dudley. He comes weekly to check on the place and make repairs. He won't stay here at night."

"And neither would yew if yew knew what was good for yew."

The voice, raspy and dry with age, came from the direction of the house behind us. Megan stiffened, and I caught a look of surprise and annoyance flickering across her face as we moved to face the owner of the voice. Her hand lightly pressed on my wrist as I instinctively reached for my revolver, pausing me and then gently urging me to drop my hand as we turned.

Megan chuckled. "Speak the devil's name and he appears."

Dudley was a bent and broken figure of a man. He was rail thin and walked with a slight limp as he approached us. I assumed he'd come around the house as silently as possible, observing us in a manner not unlike spying, and then headed out from the imposing arch of the main entrance when he was sure his appearance would be most effective. Bloody dramatics, I thought, and cried inwardly at the thought of an entire weekend spent in a house rigged up to appear haunted. I always found such parlor tricks loathsome in their baseness, for they made discerning real phenomena and their causes more difficult and that meant an increase in the chances of bodily injury, psychic scarring, death, or worse. At the end of the day, death by dismemberment (or incurring a fate worse than death) was bad for business and that cut both ways; I certainly did not want to face such a death, and dead clients can give no referrals. As the man replied to Megan, I turned and finished unpacking the trunk.

"The devil is not ta be mocked; yew should know better." Dudley raised a crooked finger and pointed. "I'll assume you are Mister and Misses Peaslee?"

"We are," I acknowledged, putting the last bag on the ground and turning around. "Zorba says that all this ghost stuff is nonsense. That everything you've heard and seen can be explained—that is, if you're not making it all up." Without turning to look, I reached back and closed the trunk with an easy pull. The metallic CLUNK emphasized my comment.

"S'all true, I swear. The devil hisself roams this house." Dudley crossed himself crudely and then spat to his side.

I grinned mockingly. "As impressive as this place is, I doubt the devil would choose to reside here—and if he did," I pointed back at Dudley, "why would you choose to stay? Unless perhaps you had reasons for keeping people away from this place?"

Dudley sneered and limped back towards the house. In a grotesque caricature of servitude, he stopped at the door and dropped into a low bow, bending deeply at the waist with one hand resting on the door handle and the other sweeping wide out to his side. Still bowing, he stepped to the side almost jauntily and smoothly pulled on the handle to the main door of the house, it creaked open, as one would expect it to. He raised his head, eyes burning, and spoke in a low tone. "By all means come inside, spend the night, spend the week. Then you tell me that I'm lying."

Megan laughed, and the sound startled us both, the old man and me, and shattered the tension of the moment. I blinked at the sound and looked at the gear we had unloaded. There were our two suitcases that I knew to be full of clothes, and then three other bags that were equipped with sundry other items that I hoped we didn't have to ever unpack. I glanced at the old man at the entryway. He had straightened and was watching us keenly, waiting to see what sort of people we were.

I picked up the heavier of the cases and looked at my wife questioningly. "You sure you want to do this?"

Megan bent down into a crouch and opened the other suitcase. She poked around for a moment and then snapped the case shut. She stood and picked up the suitcase, and replied, "We're already here, might as well go through with it." She stalked off toward the front door. I sighed and gathered the rest of the bags before following. I glanced at the entryway, at Dudley, and saw he was grinning at our approach, pleased his theatrics had worked. A moment later, we followed him into the house.

There was a small vestibule with a short set of stairs leading down a hall into the ground floor and a similar set leading up to the first floor. To the side a heavy door with a large lock seemed embedded into the very rock of the structure. Dudley stood before us, puffed up with the pride of a museum curator showing off a new exhibit. He gestured at the house around us and began his tour.

"The four stories of The Krag are divided by function," explained Dudley. "The ground floor houses a large kitchen, pantry, boiler, and various storerooms. The second floor is for entertaining and includes a dining room, butler's pantry, a billiards room, a small study attached to an ample library, and a rather large lounge that opens up to the loggia. The rear deck that overlooks the sea is accessed through the salon. The third floor holds ten bedrooms and the solarium. The tower observatory is only accessible through the loggia. The first floor of the tower constitutes the workshop, while the actual telescopes are on the upper level. The basement is divided into sections, storage mostly, but also the generator." He took the steps up to the first floor. "I've taken the liberty of putting you and your wife in the master bedroom overlooking the ocean."

"Dudley, does that lead to the basement?" I gestured at the door with the heavy lock. There was a faded design laid into the door, tarnished metal strips that ran vertically through the wood and joined the frame.

Dudley didn't even bother to look. "Yes, the stairs run through part of a cave system that riddles the cliff side. It's why the house is called The Krag."

Megan smiled ironically and spoke in a voice just loud enough for me to hear. "That is an awfully big lock."

"Things just keep getting better." I muttered back and looked at her hand. "How're the fingers?"

She flexed them for me. "A little stiff, but nothing I can't work with. Your shoulder doing better?"

"Almost completely healed. Might leave a scar, though."

Dudley was pulling ahead, still pointing out odds and ends that were of no consequence in his weary and resigned voice.

"Let's get settled and find out what is really going on around here. She hauled the case up the stairs. I followed with my own baggage.

Four steps up and we were on the second floor of the house in what appeared to be the main hall. There was a coatroom to one side, and a winding staircase leading up on the other. Before us was a large reception room that apparently hadn't been used in years. Cobwebs hung from the ceiling, and the furniture in the room was all covered with sheets, but even these had gone grey with dust. Beyond the room a corridor led down the length of the house and I could see closed doors, which I assumed led to the various rooms of the house. The walls, ceilings and floors were all made of hardwood stained a warm red and—again—inlaid with the tarnished metal strips that ran across the floor, up the walls and across the ceiling. Up close and on a larger scale, I could see that the inlaid strips were not simple straight lines, but periodically contained a number of geometric shapes including circles, triangles, pentagons and heptagons. Short lengths of metal connected the vertices of some of these shapes. I tried to find a sequence to this cross-pattern but, in the few moments I had, I could figure nothing simple out. It was an odd place, and the whole of what I was seeing gave me pause, but I thought that this might simply have been caused by the task at hand, rather than any particular sense of foreboding.

Then Megan spoke up, breaking my contemplation. "The inlay in these walls," her hand reached out and touched the metal, and then she gasped and withdrew her hand rapidly.

I took her shoulder, "Were you shocked?"

She shook her head, "No, I don't think so." She was looking at her hand. "Maybe just some static electricity." She looked up at the ceiling and around the room, taking the whole place in. "This design is so strange. The architect must have been obsessed."

"'T'weren't no architect that did the inlay Missus—that was Flux hisself. Did it all by hand. The designs are in his study," commented Dudley. "Runs through the entire house, 'cept of course the basement and the tower, ain't no wood in there."

In a dazed sort of wonder at the maniacal work Flux had done, we followed Dudley up the stairs to our accommodations.

As promised by the caretaker, the wondrous metal work continued up the stairs, and Megan reached out her hand and ran her fingertips along one circuit of it, trailing it softly as it moved up and down the wall. At the top of the stairs there was a threshold, and the inlay dove through the wall beneath the woodwork to emerge on the other side. Megan barely missed a beat, lifting her hand up on one side of the wall and bringing it back down on the other, but fully three inches higher than where it had entered the carving.

When I asked her how she had known that the inlay would be that much higher she just stopped and stared at me. "I don't know, it just seemed the proper way." I didn't pursue the question any further.

The room that Dudley brought us to was large and satisfactory, unremarkable save for the inlay that continued here as well. There was a large bed with fresh linens, and Dudley had done a yeoman's job of dusting. There was an *en suite* bathroom with a sink, shower and toilet. The windows in the bath and the bedroom both overlooked the sea but were not operational, in the sense that they were not designed to be open. They provided light and a view, but that was all. I had thought, briefly, that they were composed of decorative stained glass, but upon inspection discovered they were like the walls, riddled with that strange metallic inlay—albeit here the geometric shapes were more numerous and clustered together in a tight, almost interlocking pattern, perhaps to support the more fragile glasswork.

Dudley left us alone and Megan and I unpacked our bags.

"After we finish, do you want to explore the house?"

She looked at her watch, and then looked at me with a cocked head and annoyed eyes. "Do you mean do I want to explore the big spooky house where a man obsessed with contacting the dead once lived? Sure, bring it on," she pulled back her jacket and revealed her pistols.

"I'm not sure that those will help against ghosts."

"Are you still carrying?" She asked.

"Yes," I patted the holster underneath my arm.

"Why?"

"It's not ghosts that I'm concerned with. Zorba warned us about the students."

 The Miskatonic University Spiritualism Club

She smiled, "And barring any unforeseen developments, my pistols will work perfectly fine against students."

I snickered. "I very much doubt that you would need a gun to handle any of Zorba's students."

"And neither would you, Mister Peaslee. So, why are we both so on edge that we feel the need to carry?"

"I have the feeling that there's more going on than we're being told."

"You don't think Zorba told us everything?"

"I think Zorba is just like everybody else we've dealt with in this business," I opened the bedroom door and let her step out into the hall. "They lie. Everybody tends to lie."

Our exploration of the house was uneventful. The third floor was, as Dudley described, ten bedrooms, though one would scarcely qualify—I thought of it more as a nursery, but it was devoid of any furnishings besides the ceiling light. The other rooms were all well apportioned with double beds, dressers, assorted chairs and stools. Several had vanities with ornate mirrors. There were four other full bathrooms, each shared by the two adjoining bedrooms. At the end of the hall there was an ornate pair of glass doors both inlaid with the strange metalwork. These led to what Dudley had called the solarium. It was a huge, single open room, the roof and walls of which were made of thick glass framed by steel beams that were bolted directly into the masonry. I had a feeling that the whole structure had been a late addition to the building, that at one point this had simply been an open terrace and that the glass and metal work had been grafted on at a later date. It did its job, though; even in late December the room was quite warm. Despite this, the plants that had once thrived there were long dead, dried out husks of their former selves. Plants need more than just sunlight and space. They need water and tending to, which I doubt Dudley had ever bothered with. For some reason I felt sorry for the nearly mummified vegetation. There had been so much life in this room once, and now it was all . . .

"Dead," stated Megan. "It's all dead."

I looked around knowing she was right, but for some reason I wanted to prove her wrong, desperate to find some last vestige of life that was still holding out amongst the ashy brown leaves. I found it, of course. It was in a pot, nestled between the branches of a long dead rose bush. It was a spider, small and shiny and black, barely the size of a pinhead. It hung there in a web, surrounded by the dead bodies of its victims—flies, gnats, and mosquitos. I pointed it out to Megan.

She looked at it and sighed. "It's horrible. Like a ghoul in a cemetery, hunting down whatever visitors might wander in." She turned and walked away, leaving me alone to stare at the tiny animal that made its lonely home in the solarium, surviving as best it could in a world it didn't understand, and could never fully visualize.

The style of architecture and the inlaid metalwork continued downstairs, extending beyond the reception room and down the hall—though the rooms were obviously much more diverse in function. On the right was a large dining room with a thick black table, well used but still in good repair, that could easily seat ten, maybe even twelve, people. Behind this but to the side was a butler's pantry with a large cabinet filled with china, and a matching one for silverware. There was a large preparation table, and a dumbwaiter that I presumed led down to the kitchen. Across from the dining room was a game room dominated by a billiards table, but also with a small table for cards, and a dartboard. Next to the game room was a rather large private library. The library had only small windows across the top of the wall, and these were of dark green glass. As with most libraries, this one's collection had long outgrown its allotted space. Where possible the shelves had been pressed into double duty, but even this was insufficient and the floors around the shelves had become home to stacks of books, journals, and monographs. Some of these were readily identifiable and seemed to be related to astronomical studies, but I also saw copies of the *Journal of the Society for Psychical Research* and the *Proceedings of the American Society for Psychical Research*. Surprisingly, I saw the familiar name of Zorba printed on the spine of a thin volume and casually picked it up. It turned out to be the Doctor's graduate thesis, a series of interviews with the spiritualist Harley Warren. I returned it to the pile but made a mental note to come back for it.

Attached to the library, but also with its own door off the hall, was a small study. Where the library could have been considered the personification of overstuffed chaos, the study was the exact opposite. The desk was small and neat, with a blotter and a typewriter to one side. The windows were large and clear, though still riddled with the metallic inlay, and let in a surfeit of natural light. In one corner was a celestial globe, a golden sphere encircled by a brass ring. One whole wall, albeit the smaller one, played host to a rather singular painting. It was a scene of the night sky with a starscape filling the majority of the canvas, and two small moons in the upper right corner. It was a disquieting image for it seemed to me to show a vaguely familiar set of constellations but from a wholly unfamiliar perspective. On the frame was a brass plaque that read *The Twin Moons: Thog and Thok, from Their Sister Nithon*. The artist was not noted, but Megan recognized it immediately.

"An early piece by Basil Hallward. We study him at the Hall School. There were stories—all denied of course—that in his younger days Egyptian magic, particularly the Goddess Bast and her consort Ulthah, had infatuated Hallward. A youthful indiscretion that was quickly forgotten after Hallward began moving in more refined circles and doing portraits of the aristocracy."

Next to the dining room was a salon with several couches and a divan and a small piano in the corner. A door led to an open-air deck that overlooked the ocean. It was my first time seeing the seascape from the house. It was a dreary view. The sky was slate grey—a near mirror image to the ocean below—and both seemed equally turbulent, making the dividing line on the horizon between the rolling clouds and the roiling ocean difficult to define. The two churned against each other, with only a few winter gulls floating in the sky like lonely travelers lost in a vast chaotic nothingness. I wondered what it must be like to be a sailor on such a sea, to be lost in so much alien gray, so far from home or any hospitable equivalent. Taking the view in for only a moment before moving on, I was nonetheless left with a disturbing question after seeing that churning vista: Was it any wonder that some men went mad?

Where the salon had been a formal space, the lounge we found next door was less so, and the furnishings were appropriately less showy, and even a bit tatty in places. The space was modest, rather comfortable, and decorated with artifacts that invoked the local history of the town, particularly its function as a summer destination for Arkham's well-to-do. Adorning the walls were a dozen or so original paintings—mostly seascapes, but also a few of the town from what seemed to be the perspective of the beach or from just offshore—all done in bright colors, light pastels stressing the bright and light feeling of the area. These were all signed by the same artist, P. Flux, who I assumed to be a relative of the previous owner.

The two ends of the lounge were anchored by a semicircular loggia that wrapped around the stone tower that formed the base of the observatory. It was from here that a large copper door provided access to the tower. The door had been properly mounted, and therefore, despite its size, swung open quite effortlessly. It was in many ways similar to the bulkhead doors I had seen in various oceangoing vessels; after we passed through, the closure of the door released an audible hiss that seemed to indicate that a seal of some sort had been achieved. The inside of the lower part of the tower consisted of bare rock both in the walls and floor, into which iron rods had been drilled to support an encircling staircase and the upper level of wooden planks. The lower space was a single room populated by a number of wide and thick worktables and tool benches. The work surfaces were covered with a plethora of small machines, electronics, and tools arranged in an orderly manner. Every tool was in its place and all the equipment seemed to be aligned and in working order, if a little outdated. There was one thing that was very odd, and both Megan and I noticed it almost immediately. Nowhere in this part of the house was there any of the metallic inlay, and the reason for that was quite obvious—doing that kind of work in this section would have required working into stone, rather than wood. Instead, there was a thin mesh of wire netting that had been hung up along the walls and doors and windows. It was even draped around the stairs.

As I said, the stairs leading up wrapped around the interior wall, spiraling up such that the end overhung the beginning, but only for a few yards. There was no rail on the outer edge so the climb up was made slightly more harrowing than needed, though truth be told the stairs were wide and well-constructed and groaned only a little as we ascended. Closer to the top we noted that the floor above us contained a trap door, which we assumed was for moving equipment from the lower level to the upper. As I mounted the upper level, that assumption was confirmed by a large winch suspended from the rafters and the presence of equipment of such size that it could not have been brought up in any other way. The centerpiece of the room was what appeared to be a kind of telescope, approximately twenty-four inches in diameter and twenty feet long, that almost jutted out of the metal dome above. The telescope was mounted on a pair of tracks that allowed it to swing a full three-hundred-and-sixty degrees around the room, and then be locked into place with a small hand brake. The dome with its iris opening was similarly mounted on a track that allowed for the same range of movement. Megan noted that both mechanisms appeared to be operated by hand cranks, meaning that one would have to be quite strong to reposition the dome. One would also have to take care that the winch was well secured, for movement of any of the three risked a collision between the hook and the telescope. Most interesting was the fact that, try as we might, neither Megan or I could find an eyepiece—rather, the end of the telescope was connected to a series of wires that ran to a bank of equipment, the front of which was festooned with a number of switches, knobs and dials.

We were just about to investigate further when we heard the sound of a car engine coming down the drive. A quick look out a window showed us that a sedan and a small truck were arriving. I saw Mr. Dudley outside, waving about and trying to direct their vehicles to an area he deemed fit for them to park in. I was treated to a brief but very complex waltz of man and machinery as I watched the complicated affair below. We left our post at the window and, after a brief discussion, we started down to the main hall as we deemed it best to go down and meet the Zorba and the students we had been hired to protect.

As we came through the main door, we could hear Doctor Zorba barking directions.

"The stairs at the far end of the property lead down the cliff, and to be honest they're a real mess. So, everybody stays off the beach." He paused and looked at the five students that were mulling about wondering what to do. "Plato, you and Elaine get the groceries into the kitchen. Cross and Loren can deliver the suitcases to the rooms. Delambre and Quinton, you can begin setting up the equipment in the main hall."

Dudley had his hand out and was asking for the keys to the truck. Zorba dangled them in the air for a moment. "Plato," he called out without looking, "do we have everything off the truck?"

An older student with dark, curly hair did a quick survey of the boxes and luggage they had unloaded and then nodded. It took him a split second to realize that his father couldn't hear a nod. "Yessir."

Zorba dropped the keys into the grizzled old hand. "Sunday, Mr. Dudley, and I expect you bright and early."

The old man's eyes narrowed. "I'll be here, Doctor, and I sincerely hope that yew and yer students are here when I come back."

He hobbled his way to the truck, climbed in and drove off.

Zorba saw us and shrugged apologetically. "University vehicle. The motor pool manager wouldn't let me keep it for the entire week. Something about students and holiday joyrides."

An hour later, after we had moved all the equipment and luggage inside, we were gathered in the kitchen for lunch. Somebody had made a spicy sausage and lentil soup. It wasn't up to Mrs. Kreitner's standards—it could have used a bit more seasoning—but it was tasty in its own right, and satisfying on a chilly December day. There was tea as well, with a hint of cranberries. As we sat around drinking, Doctor Zorba made introductions.

"Gentlemen, these are the people that are going to babysit us over the next few days. Robert Peaslee is a former military man and police detective. The rather severe woman next to him is his wife Doctor Megan Halsey, the daughter of the famed Doctor Allan Halsey who died serving the city of Arkham."

A voice from the crowd cut off the doctor, calling out: "And the heir to the Griffith family fortune. She might not look it but she's one of the richest women in Essex County."

The speaker was one of the students: a thin, distinguished looking young man with perfectly coiffed hair and an impeccable manicure.

Doctor Zorba was obviously annoyed and he, almost sarcastically, now pivoted his introduction to include this young upstart and the other students. "This somewhat rude young man is Frederick Loren, a rather mediocre business student. What he lacks in social graces and scholarly aptitude he makes up with access to his family fortune, and a rather macabre sense of humor." The indicated youth raised his cup in a mock toast.

"Next to him is law student Russell Quinton. He's from Boston, but don't hold that against him. The dashing young man in the navy-blue sweater is my protégé, Dick Cross." Zorba let the young man give me a two-fingered salute before moving on. "The young man with the French accent is Francois Delambre, perhaps the best electrical engineering student

Miskatonic University has ever produced. The same could be said of Elaine Zachirides, though her field is anthropology, in the vein of Margaret Murray. And, last but not least, is my son, the President of the Miskatonic University Spiritualism Club, Plato Zorba." The kid was the splitting image of his father, just a quarter century younger.

Megan smiled sweetly, and then cut to the chase. "You've made the introductions, Doctor Zorba. Now what do we do next?"

"Well, it is Christmas Eve. We have to set up some equipment, and Elaine has promised to prepare a sumptuous feast for tonight. I suggest the two of you take the remaining daylight hours and familiarize yourself with the grounds. After that you can do the same with the house. Supper will be at . . ."

"Eight," concluded Elaine in a rather crisp and clear midwestern tone. "Dinner will be at eight."

"And after that," interjected Fred Loren, "a ghost story."

The members of the Miskatonic University Spiritualism Club laughed.

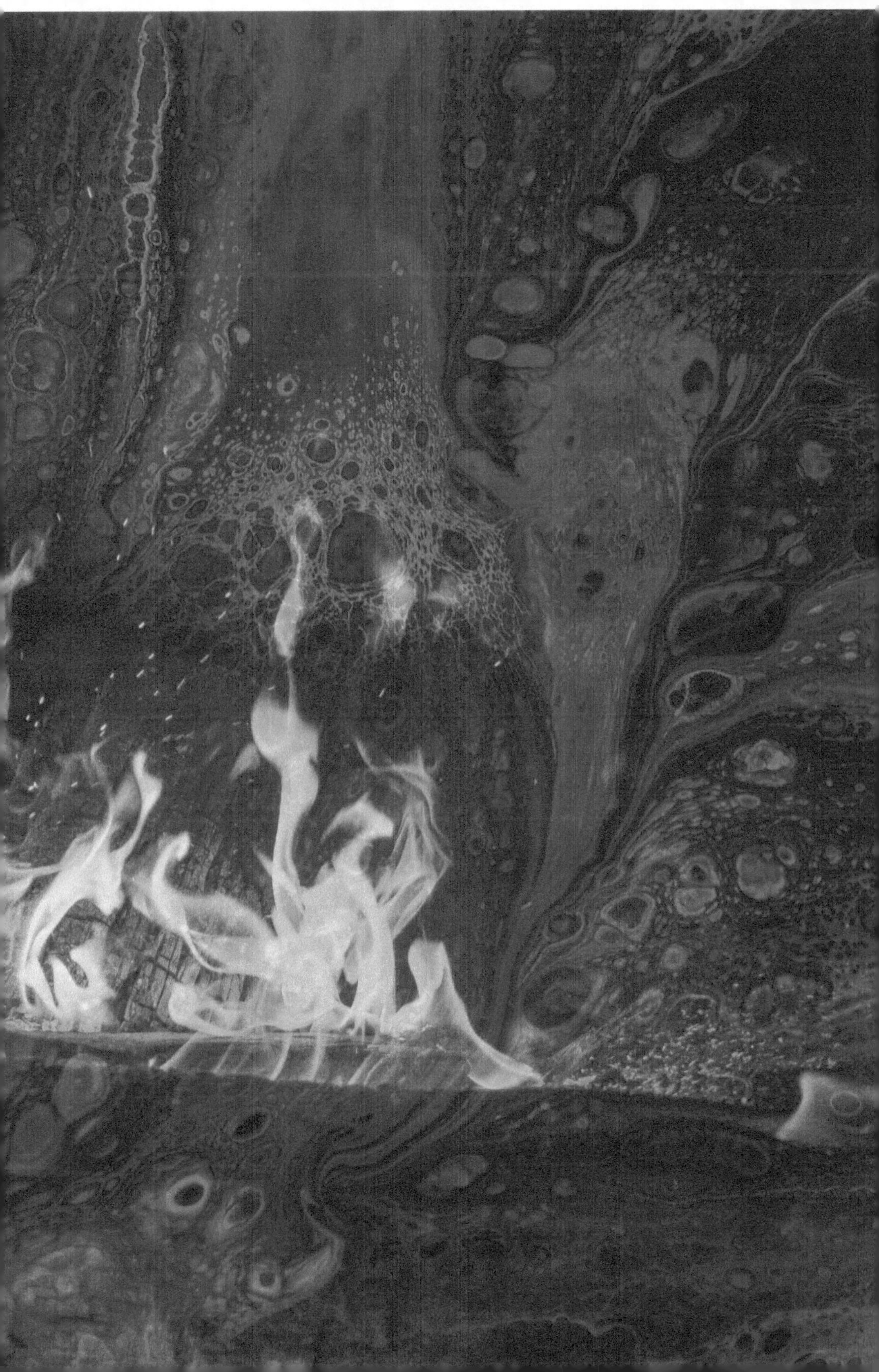

December 24, 1928
– Evening –

Dinner was surprisingly excellent, a spread that offered a shockingly tender goose paired with salad of preserved cranberry gelatin and winter greens, and clams and walnuts glazed in maple syrup. After the meal, the students tended to the dishes while we sat in the salon where Plato had built a fire and Delambre—who was not French, but rather from Quebec—had provided a bottle of brandy. The sounds of the ocean breeze whistling against the house and the waves crashing against the cliff evoked a natural eeriness that set the mood for what was to follow.

Doctor Zorba swirled his snifter close to the light of the fire, letting the heat warm the brandy. He took a sniff and then a small sip and smiled. "Mister Loren, I do believe you promised us a ghost story."

"A ghost story on Christmas Eve?" It seemed to me somewhat incongruous.

"On the contrary, Mister Peaslee," suggested Cross, "ghost stories at Christmas are a British tradition. Dickens' *A Christmas Carol* may be the most famous, but there are a plethora of other tales written about Christmas ghosts. And Christmas is ripe for telling such tales. It is the end of the year; the days have grown short, and the nights long. A suitable time for spirits to find the thin spots between this world and the next and cross over. Which is why Loren promised us a story."

Loren—occupying a wing-backed chair upholstered in a paisley pattern nearest to the fire—took a drag off his cigarette and leaned forward, his own glass of brandy in his hands between his knees. "Indeed, I did, but if you recall it was I who told last week's tale, concerning the invisible monster of Passamaquoddy, and the week before that Delambre told the legend of Dr. Charriere of Quebec."

"And before that I discussed the legend of Belasco House," chimed in the younger Zorba.

"I did Hill House," offered Quinton.

All eyes turned to Richard Cross, "Sorry friends, I did Rose Red in early November."

Doctor Zorba turned and looked at Elaine Zachirides, who sat to the side of the room distractedly peering out one of the windows. She started when Zorba addressed her, the contents of her own snifter sloshed around. "Isn't it true, my dear, that you haven't regaled us since All Hallows' Eve?"

The young woman thought about it for a moment and then nodded. She set down her glass and stood up. She was a thin woman, close to gaunt, but she seemed at ease, almost in command, as she took center stage in front of the fireplace. She cleared her throat and began to speak.

"Two decades or so ago, a woman was hired to work as a maid for a man who lived alone in a big house overlooking the sea. She was not a beautiful woman but she wasn't ugly, either. He was not an old man, nor was he young. The child he had had with his wife had died, and in their mourning, they had grown apart, and then slowly came to loathe each other. And so, the wife had left the man, leaving him to ramble around in a house that was too big for him and filled with memories of his wife and child and the love he had once known."

She paused, picked up her glass, turned to Loren and waved him out of the chair. As he vacated the spot she sat down, took a sample from her own snifter and then began her tale in earnest. "Every day the woman came to the house; she came along the beach, for that was the shortest and easiest path, and climbed the stairs that led up the cliff to the house that overlooked the sea. She came in fair weather and foul, in summer and winter. She came when his mood was poor and he could do little more than get out of bed and wander down to breakfast in his dressing gown, and she came on the days when the melancholy lifted, and he could finally return to work. She came every day, even after he no longer needed her. She came and made him breakfast and packed his lunch. She came and cleaned his house and did his laundry and made him dinner. And after a year, when she decided that she no longer needed to come every day, that he was in such a condition that he could take care of himself, he told her no, that he needed her to come each and every day.

"It was not long after that the two were spied walking on the beach in the evening hand in hand. This was not a surprise, and the townsfolk all agreed that the pair made an attractive couple. Indeed, it was noted that for the first time in many years the man was seen to smile and heard to laugh. The only obstacle in their way was the man's wife. She had left him, yes, but neither had moved to legally divorce. In fact, it seemed that both had good reasons to remain married. Something to do with codicils in various wills in both families that united their business interests, the undoing of which would leave them both destitute. So the separated couple remained married, and the man and the woman who had found love together never could. This, however, did not stop them from behaving as such."

I watched as all the young men leaned forward, their interest suddenly piqued. "I won't bore you with the sordid details," I could almost hear the other students sigh in disappointment, "but eventually and inevitably and not unexpectedly, the woman was with child. This made both of them very happy and arrangements were made for her to finally move into the house.

This plan did not sit well with the man's wife. Even though she had left the marriage voluntarily, she accused the woman of being a *magissa*— a sorceress—who had bewitched the man. Lawyers were called, and the case was discussed and Judge Zellaby ruled, albeit reluctantly."

She paused and took another sip of her drink. "A fund was set up to provide for both mother and child; however this did not sit well with the woman, who continued to come by the beach to the house only to find the gate up the stairs locked, and the man sadly staring at her from a window. She came every day, pausing only for a few weeks toward the end of her pregnancy. After the child was born, she resumed her routine, and every day she walked the beach with the child swathed in a blanket, and every day she stopped at the locked gate and showed the child to the sad man in the window. For years this went on, and the child grew strong and she learned to walk on the beach. She stumbled at first, and was quite a bit slower than her mother, but eventually she learned to keep pace and keep the routine."

Another pause and another sip of brandy. "Then one day, after almost fifteen years—this would have been in 1919—the woman and her child stopped walking along the beach. The woman had succumbed to the influenza epidemic and left her child to be raised by her grandparents, but not before making her daughter promise to continue the daily walks. And so the young woman walked to the beach alone and watched as her father mourned the death of yet another loved one."

She took a breath, and Doctor Zorba took the opportunity to interject. "Elaine, do you really want to be telling this story?"

"Oh, yes, Doctor," she replied with a touch of condescension. "For nearly three years that young woman followed in her mother's footsteps, going every day at the same time, just as her mother had done. Watching her father become a sad old man. Then one day her father was not where he should have been. He was in another room, and instead of looking sad he seemed almost overjoyed to see her. He stood there in his fancy red dressing gown and waved for her to come up. She found this peculiar, as the terms of the judge's ruling and her trust had made it clear that they could never meet. So, she ignored it and went about her day. It went like that for a week. She would walk to his house and he would be there in his dressing gown waving to her imploring her to come up, but she would just shake her head and turn around and walk back home."

Elaine finished her drink. "Then, on the eighth day he wasn't there. Nor was he there on the ninth day, or the tenth. She thought at first that maybe the man had grown weary of their ritual. That whatever had bound him to her mother did not hold the same strength with her daughter, and so she did nothing; but after an entire week had gone by and she had seen not a hair of movement in the house, she called the authorities and expressed her concerns."

An evil smile crept across Elaine's face as she entered the final phase of the story. "The police had to force their way in—the mail had built up for weeks, and the stench from dirty dishes and rotten food was horrendous. Of the house's residents there was not a single trace. The police suggested that the house had been abandoned for more than two weeks."

Francois Delambre leaned forward, "Two weeks—then who had she seen in the window?"

Elaine smiled. "That was the same question that the police asked the young woman when they brought her in for questioning. They thought perhaps she had murdered the man and then hidden the body, waiting for time to deal with the corpse before reporting him missing. But she was steadfast in her account, and there was one tiny problem with the idea that she had murdered the man."

"And what was that?" begged Richard Cross, who seemed enraptured by the tale.

She turned and walked to the window and looked down at the beach. "As I have said, the police had to break in. All the windows and doors had been locked, bolted from the inside. If it was murder, then it was what they call 'an impossible crime' or 'locked-room mystery' such as those recorded by Le Fanu, Poe, Leroux, and most recently by S. S. Van Dine."

Megan glanced at me, for I had personal history with Van Dine— well, more with Philo Vance than Van Dine. I just nodded to acknowledge the connection.

"It's a rather weak story, isn't it, Elaine?" Russell Quinton was suddenly on his feet. His comment felt smug and gloating. "What I mean is that it's obviously just a sad story of two lovers torn apart by circumstance and their illegitimate child with the story of the ghost tacked on at the end. There's no real way to prove any of it as a real haunting."

Doctor Zorba was suddenly standing as well, and he put a hand on Quinton's shoulder. "Russell you shouldn't . . ."

"It's all right Doctor, he's right. On the face of it, there is nothing that cannot be dismissed as being made up or simply embellished through the years. It's his job to be skeptical." She reached out and touched the glass. "But I've left out a few critical details. The house that I'm speaking of, it's this house. The man who vanished was Jackson Flux. He died in this room." She turned slowly around, the moon and the sea silhouetting her. "And I am his illegitimate daughter."

And with that she crumpled like a doll, collapsing to the floor.

The others thought it was part of the story and laughed. Loren went so far as to begin applauding. It was only after she hadn't responded that young Plato Zorba dropped his glass and ran to her side. The glass bounced against the stonework and then shattered into dozens of curved and sharp shards.

"I'm fine," she told young Zorba as he helped her up. "Just a little light-headed," she added as she reached her feet.

What happened next seemed a bit contrived—in fact, were I not a witness to the event I would almost have thought it faked. Plato helped Elaine into a chair and then turned, saying he was going to get her some water. He took a step forward and the heel of his left shoe came down on a shard of glass. Plato reacted poorly, stumbled, and fell to the floor himself. Fortunately—or unfortunately, depending on how you look at it—he was able to get his hands out in front of him to break his fall, but his hands encountered more glass. When he recovered, one very large shard was embedded in his palm. The bleeding began almost immediately and was quite severe.

Elaine jumped to his rescue, grabbing a napkin off the table and wrapping his hand with it to stem the flow. There then ensued a bit of discussion about what should be done. Both Elaine and his father wanted to take the boy to the hospital, but the young man kept refusing, suggesting that it would heal on its own. Finally—frustrated with the situation—Megan stepped forward, grabbed the boy's wrist and took a look herself. A moment later I was sent to get her medical bag. The boy needed five stitches; something that Megan was more than capable of doing. Afterwards she treated the wound with Merc-urochrome and properly bandaged it. She gave him a handful of aspirin for the pain. With the excitement over and the wound taken care of, the students all began to drift out of the room. Elaine helped Plato along the way.

As she left, the elder Zorba turned to both of us. He seemed about to apologize, but instead walked over to where Elaine had been staring out the window and looked down at the beach. He mumbled something; I couldn't be sure exactly what it was, but it might have been "Welcome home, Elaine, and Merry Christmas."

Outside, it had begun to snow.

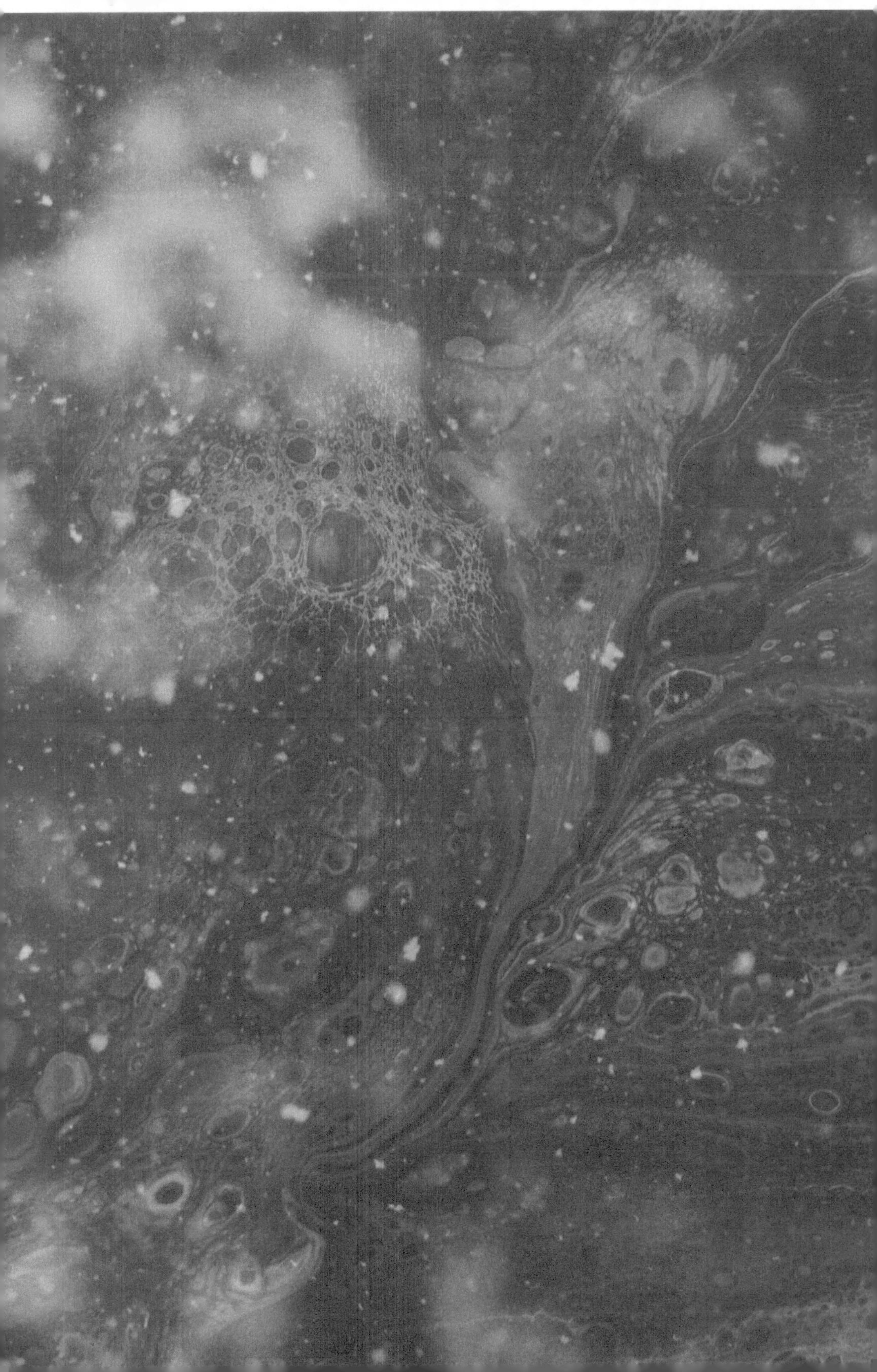

December 25, 1928

Come morning, the snow was still falling. In the still places, where the wind wasn't a factor, I thought that perhaps it was six inches deep, made of the finest powder I had ever seen laid out across the New England landscape. In fact, it was safe to wager that the scene to the north was so perfectly representative of the idyllic New England winter it would have made Currier and Ives salivate. To the east, however, was a nightmare worthy of Paul Nash or Dali. The falling snow had mixed with the sea spray coming up over the cliff and left behind a frozen hellscape. The whole seaward side of the house had become encased in ropy tendrils of thick grey ice. To the east, the wind had driven the snow into deep piles against the cars and across the drive and the front of the house.

"Snowed in," commented Megan as we surveyed the situation from an upstairs window. "If the gate is like this, we might be stranded for a few days." She craned her neck to see around the window casing. "Phone lines look like they're down as well. We might well thank Mister Dudley for leaving us all that firewood." We headed downstairs, following the smell of coffee.

Doctor Zorba finished his coffee and put his cup down on the kitchen counter. "There should be enough oil for the furnace to last a few days."

"And there seems to be a sufficient amount of gas for the stove," offered Elaine as she proffered a carafe of coffee to those of us gathered around the table. The only one missing was young Plato Zorba, who—we learned as Elaine poured the coffee—was still recovering from his wound, and had been delivered breakfast in his room by Elaine, who was obviously sweet on the boy.

We drank our coffee and ate the sparse spread of toast and jam and some oatmeal. One by one the others left until it was just myself, Megan, Elaine and Zorba.

"So, Doctor Zorba, what are the club's plans for today?" asked Megan.

There was a furtive glance between Zorba and Elaine. "Delambre is going to set up some equipment, including several recording compasses, some radios tuned to unused frequencies, and something he calls the Evil Eye, which uses invisible ultraviolet light and sensors to trigger cameras to automatically take pictures and sound an alarm if something moves in a room."

That seemed unhelpful to me. "Aren't photographs pretty useless until they are developed? It won't help knowing that something moved until you know who or what that is."

Zorba nodded. "My son is something of a photography buff, and all of our cameras have built-in portable wet darkrooms, as invented by Shlafrock several years ago. It still takes a few minutes, but we will have the developed pictures within a useful enough time frame to see what triggered the sensor. I and the other students will be looking through Flux's documents trying to find any records or notes suggesting he actually succeeded in contacting the dead."

"And what do you expect us to be doing during this time?" I wanted to make sure I knew exactly what we were being paid for.

"Just stay out of our way," Zorba said. "Explore the house or read a book. Play cards. Unless something goes wrong, we really won't need you, and I don't expect anything to go wrong."

"There is of course tonight's séance," added Elaine.

"Yes, I had forgotten that. You're welcome to attend if you wish." Zorba looked back and forth at us and smiled.

We agreed to watch, but when we didn't take the hint that he wanted us to leave the room, both he and Elaine finished what they were doing and bid us farewell.

We finished our breakfast and began to wander about the house, this time taking more notice of the details. After a time we wound up in the library, where I browsed the shelves, and Megan took a closer look at the metal inlay that decorated the floors and walls.

"What a queer design," she said, pointing out the geometry.

I nodded in agreement. "It reminds me of some Amish decor, but now that I see it up close, I'm not sure that it has anything to do with them."

Megan peered at it and then shifted her position to get a better look. "I think it's meant to represent a kind of geometric progression. The first shape is a triangle, then a pentagon, then a heptagon. The next figure has eleven sides, and then this one has thirteen. The one here at the crest has nineteen, then the whole thing begins to go back down in the same progression. All odd numbers."

"And all prime numbers."

"I hadn't noticed that."

Megan reached out to touch the wall but then pulled back quickly. She cupped her bare hand in the other. "It shocked me."

I reached out with and tried it for myself; I could feel what she was talking about. "I think it's just static, maybe because of the cold and our clothes."

Megan shrugged off the mild shock and then wandered over to the bookshelves. "Anything here of concern that we should deal with?" She was referring to our practice of finding and destroying volumes and documents that we deemed dangerous. It was a practice we had surreptitiously instituted after determining that the authorities—in this case the librarians and professors at Miskatonic University—were not responsible enough in limiting access to such things. The death of Walter Gilman and the Dunwich Horror being the most obvious cases, but one could not ignore that they allowed Herbert West and his colleagues to pursue less than healthy paths of research. If the old guard wasn't going to control access, then we would take what steps that we could.

"Not at first glance. There's a Witch House edition of Azor Sparhawk's *Observations of Mars*, but that's just a collection of drawings of the Martian canal system, mostly innocuous. The same can be said of the copy of *The Dynamics of an Asteroid*. *Kryptographik* sounds threatening but is just a book on cryptography. This, however," I picked up a thin volume, "is Lobachevsky's *Pangeometry*; it's a treatise on non-Euclidean geometry written in Russian. If I remember correctly, Gilman had studied this. Might be something to look at."

Megan took it from me and flipped it open. "Or it could be just a textbook of very high-level math." She closed it and put it back on the shelf. "I feel like we're being kept in the dark. The society is here to hunt a ghost, but Zorba is clear that he doesn't believe in them. And it's obvious that Zorba knew Elaine, who clearly believes in ghosts, was linked to the house. They're setting up all this equipment—at least some of them are— what is everybody else doing?"

"Should we force the issue?"

Megan sighed. "Not yet. It's all been pretty harmless—annoying but harmless. But the first sign of trouble, we push back."

Of course, I agreed with her. I thought for sure that trouble would come during the séance. Imagine my surprise when it came hours earlier, just before dinner.

From what I can gather, the vast majority of the club were scattered throughout the house going through papers, books and equipment. Plato Zorba was in the kitchen cooking, while Elaine was in the dining room setting the table. It was apparent to both of us that there was something between the two of them—or perhaps there was just the potential for something. Either way, they seemed to always be involved in something together, even when they weren't physically close.

Megan and I were on the upper level just getting ready to come down for dinner when we heard Elaine scream. It was an ear-piercing scream that seemed to echo through the halls. It was a scream filled with terror, and it chilled me to my core. I froze for a moment, but Megan—who, as a woman, was slightly more immune to panic than I—grabbed her guns and dashed through the door. Her actions spurred me on, and I was only a moment behind her, catching up on the stairs.

We were the first to reach the dining room, with Plato charging in from the kitchen behind us. We all saw the same thing. Elaine had thrown herself against the windows, pinned like a bug, a look of sheer terror on her face, her eyes huge, her mouth open, but no longer screaming—though it seemed she was trying. Fear had stolen her voice, taken it and kept it from her, like a child steals another's plaything. She was trying to get it back, mouthing words or sounds, but nothing would come out; her voice was just a silent void and somehow that made things worse.

Plato tried to push through us to reach her, but Megan put her arm out and held him back. With her other hand, the one with a gun, she gestured toward the table where a sudden movement drew my eye. What I saw should have been impossible.

The tablecloth was floating above the table, at least part of it was. It was draped over something, it was as if an animal was standing on the table and the tablecloth had been thrown over top of it, except we could see under the cloth, and there was nothing there—nothing at all. But the cloth was draped over something—something large and oblong. At least, I thought so. I only caught sight of this half-glimpsed shape for a moment before Delambre rushed into the room, grabbed a chair and used it as a makeshift weapon to club the thing. The chair hit the tablecloth and then both were driven by Delambre into the table. It was as if the thing that had been under the fabric had vanished completely, but along the edges the sheet still hung in the air, drifting down slowly, as if whatever had been supporting it was now gone.

Delambre looked confused and embarrassed. "You saw that, right?" He wasn't talking to anyone in particular. "What was that?" His head swung back and forth from one person to the next. "What was that!"

The only answer came from Elaine herself, whose voice finally returned: "*Kallikantzaros! Kallikantzaros!*" Plato ran to her and she buried her head in his shoulder and began to weep.

Megan's holstered her guns. "Everyone stay calm. Getting agitated isn't going to help the situation." She turned and looked at Elaine. "Elaine, what was it you saw?"

"It was a *Kallikantzaroi*—a Christmas goblin." Elaine closed her eyes in shame and she pressed her head into Plato's chest as she spoke. "My mother would tell me about them when I was a child."

"A Christmas goblin—you mean like a Krampus or a Zwarte Piet?" suggested Delambre. The others began entering the room to see what the hullabaloo was. None seemed particularly shocked by the fact that we were discussing goblins.

"In a way," admitted Elaine, "but the Kallikantzaroi aren't associated with Saint Nicholas. According to legend they work deep in the Earth, mining and cutting away at the roots of the world tree. It is only during Christmas that they supposedly come to the surface to trouble mortals. They don't go back underground until the Epiphany on January the sixth."

"And what exactly do these Kallikantzaroi look like?" Inquired Doctor Zorba.

Elaine shrugged. "Descriptions vary. They are always black, with tufts of stiff hair scattered all over their bodies, which can be animal-like or human. They have multi-jointed legs and arms, usually noted as similar to those of goats or birds. When I saw that thing underneath the tablecloth, I finally understood what the stories were trying to describe. Unusual for subterranean goblins, they have wings and can fly. Oh, and they are mostly invisible. At least that's how my mother described them."

I looked at Elaine Zachirides. "Your mother was accused of being a *magissa*—a witch—wasn't she?"

Elaine glared back at me, "My mother was no more a witch than I am."

"That doesn't answer the question."

Plato Zorba, appearing both fearful and irate, looked down at the trembling woman he protectively clutched and then he looked back at us and shouted out, "How are we supposed to defend ourselves against something like that? We need to get out of here!"

"Calm yourself, Plato," commented Loren. "In case you've forgotten, we're snowed in. Besides, nobody has gotten hurt, and we still have a lot of house to explore."

Plato turned on his classmate, "It's always about money for you, isn't it?"

Loren grinned evilly. "Why is it that it's always people who don't have money that complain about other people being preoccupied with money?" He raised his glass to mock Plato. "Would you like an incentive to stay? I could swing a hundred dollars without much trouble."

"That's enough, Loren," barked Quinton. "You're dangerously close to crossing the line of decency."

"We all need to calm down," added Cross. "We've all had a shock, and we're reacting accordingly. We need to nip this in the bud before the incident becomes any more exaggerated."

"What does that mean?" Asked Plato, his cheeks filling with crimson rage and his voice hot with anger. I sensed a fight brewing.

"Well," Cross assumed a kind of superior stance, "it seems obvious to me that Elaine has a significant amount of anxiety over being in this house, and I think that's what contributed to her hallucination."

"Her hallucination—we all saw it!" Countered Plato, but there was a hint of doubt now, or maybe the hope of doubt.

"Did we?" Cross folded his hands together and steepled his fingers. "Or were we influenced by Elaine's hysteria? Did we see anything at all, or just what we expected to see once Elaine started screaming?"

The question went unanswered as the whole club just sat there in stunned silence, mulling over what Cross had just said. Cross had planted the seed of doubt, and that was enough. All of them were now questioning what they had seen—or thought they had seen. Megan and I included. After all, all we had seen was a sheet floating in the air.

Megan walked over to Elaine and took her hands. "All of you need to calm down. Plato and Delambre, finish setting up your equipment. The rest of you, get some sleep, and we'll sort things out in the morning." She looked Elaine in the eyes and squeezed her hands. "I'll look after Elaine tonight."

"And," she said loudly, catching the attention of everyone gathered there. She made eye contact with each member of the room before saying, "There will be no séance tonight. Go back to your quarters as soon as possible and stay there until morning. You'll be useless without sleep, so make sure you get some rest."

I looked away and out the window, trying to see the sea, to lose myself in its calming surface. But the view was obscured; the glass was covered with frost. The rest of the world seemed lost behind the pale, cold wall of ice that had encased the rear of the house. And we, it seemed, were trapped inside.

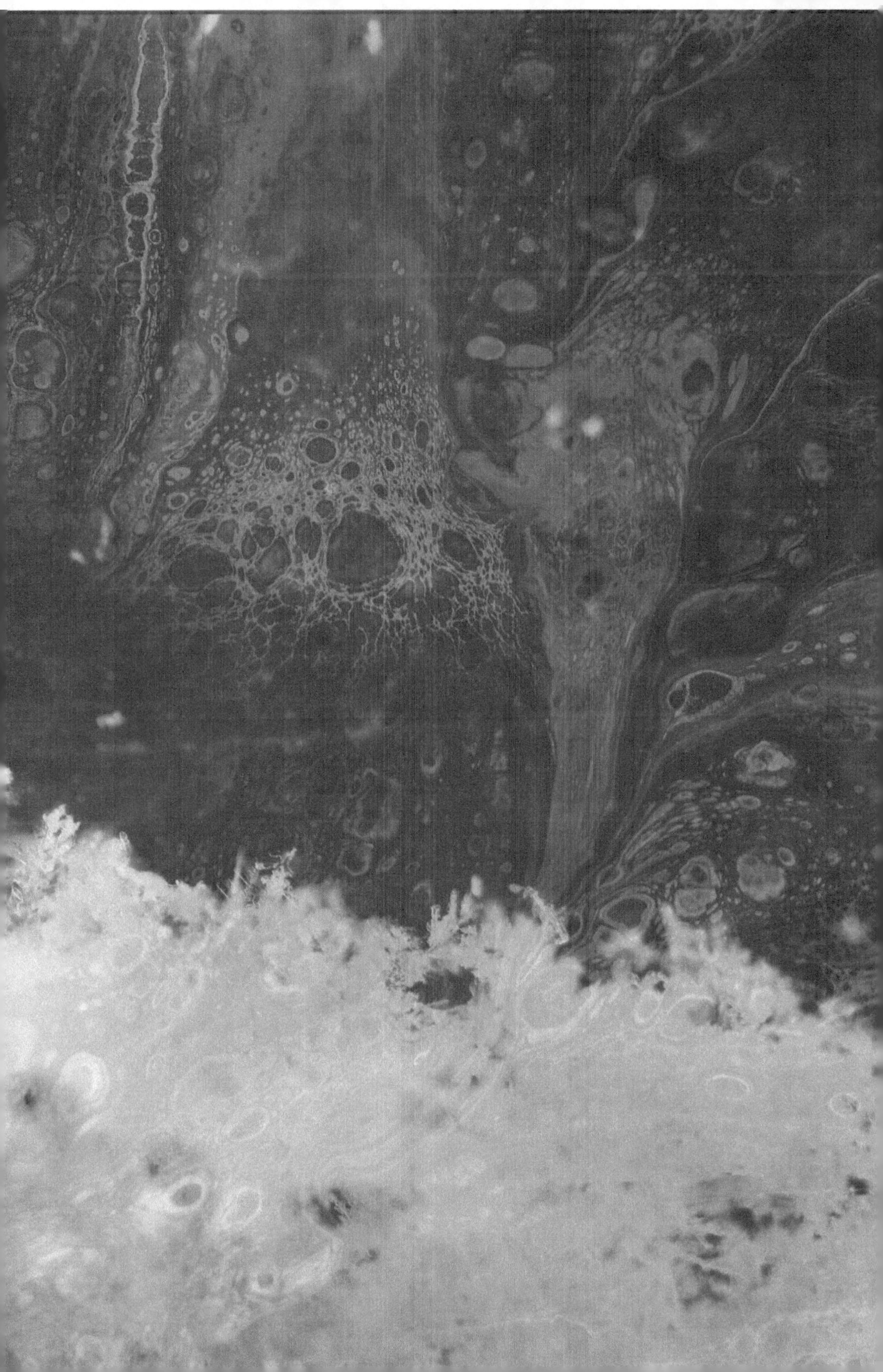

December 26, 1928

It was almost nine in the morning when we realized that Quinton hadn't come out of his room. Breakfast, as prepared by Plato, was well on its way to getting cold. Plato denied it, but I could see that he was feeling frustrated, even a little disrespected. He was pacing back and forth. All the dishes were washed and dried, and he had wiped down the counter three times. Megan gave me that look that said that I should do something. I took a swig of bad coffee, put my cup down and volunteered to go check on him.

Even at the top of the stairs I could tell something was amiss. The air was wrong. Some people will talk about how the air can be electric—charged with anticipation or excitement. This was the opposite of that. The air was dead, still, thin, drained of life, as if it wasn't there at all. I instinctively pulled my gun. It felt good in my hand, comfortable, it gave me a sense of security. Whether that was real or imagined didn't matter, since the war a gun in my hand had made me feel just a touch safer.

Quinton's room was at the far end of the hall, but even from a distance I could see the door and I could see it moving, as if a summer breeze was blowing on a screen door or a loose window. The door was slowly moving back and forth, banging in its frame. *Tap. Tap, tap. Tap. Tap, tap.* I moved my feet, propelling myself through the thin dead air. Forcing myself forward, inch by inch, step by step, stride by stride toward that terrible beat. *Tap. Tap, tap. Tap. Tap, tap.*

With each step the noise grew louder, as did my sense of overwhelming dread. Now it was like a hammer on a chisel. *TAP. Tap, tap. TAP.* I drove myself forward through malaise and through cacophony and through the sonic jabs, but all I really wanted to do was turn around and call for Megan, she was better at these things than me, more steadfast, more resolved, more resilient. She was a rock, fearless in the face of the terrible unknown. And if ever there was something terrible and unknown, it was here in this house and behind that door.

The door that was in front of me, where some unseen force beat out a demon tattoo using the door and its frame. *TAP! TAP, TAP. TAP. TAP, Tap!* My hand reached out and I forced it to take the knob. I wasn't frightened—there was nothing to be afraid of. And yet, I was shaking. My hand was trembling. The metal was cold, almost freezing but I held it tight and pulled the door forward, determined to stop that damned drumming. The door jerked in my grip, pulling against me like a fish on a line. But I pulled it tight and the door shut and held. I paused for a moment, waiting for it to wrench itself out of my hand. When it didn't, I turned the knob, feeling the latch disengage and the lock release.

I closed my eyes as I pushed the door open and steeled myself for whatever I might encounter. There was a blast of cold wind and the rhythmic noise of waves crashing on the beach below. I opened my eyes, prepared for anything. The morning sun was shining through the window, obliterating all the shadows in the room. The cold wind and sounds of the sea had the same source: in the course of the night a floor lamp had fallen over and broken a pane of the window. That was all. Nothing monstrous or soul shattering—just an empty room with a broken window, with the salt air blowing in.

I let out a sigh of relief and holstered my gun as I scanned the room. It was just a room, an empty room—nothing more, nothing less. There in the corner was Quinton's suitcase, and over the back of the chair were his pants and jacket. I peeked into the bathroom, but that was unoccupied as well. I sat down on the bed and let the cool salt air wash over me while

I wondered: where had Russell Quinton disappeared to?

We spent an hour searching the house, but to no avail. Eventually we just met back in the kitchen and tried to understand what had happened.

Richard Cross went for the obvious explanation. "He left," he gestured with a cigarette in the direction of the front door. "It's as simple as that. He either got fed up with all this nonsense or got scared and walked out to the road."

"Unfortunately, no," Megan shook her head. "I've looked at the front yard from the second story—there are no tracks in the snow. None from the house, and none down the road. It's an unspoiled landscape. Quinton didn't leave."

Cross dismissed that idea quickly. "He went out the back and took the stairs down to the beach."

Megan's eyes narrowed. "I thought of that. The gate is locked at the top of the cliff, the key is still on the hook. Besides, the stairs are covered in ice. To go down that way would be foolhardy."

"But it could be done," argued Cross. "Couldn't it?"

"Yes, but Quinton didn't leave that way, and I'm a hundred percent sure he never left the house." I placed his suitcase on the table.

Cross waved the evidence away, "That proves nothing. He just didn't want to carry it through the snow. It would have weighed him down. There's nothing in there he needed."

I laid Quinton's coat on the table beside the suitcase, and then his boots. "Would he have left these behind as well?"

Cross slumped back in his chair, finally beaten by indisputable logic and supporting evidence.

"Mister and Misses Peaslee," Doctor Zorba seemed rather perturbed. "May I have a word in private?"

Megan wasn't having any of it. "I'm sure whatever you have to say to us can be said in front of the students."

Zorba sighed in noticeable frustration, but Megan gave him a look that said *get on with it.*

"The University hired your firm to protect the students. In the first two days, one student has been injured, and another student has vanished. I have to say that performance has not matched expectations."

I could see Megan was about to say things she would regret, so I put my hand on her shoulder and tried to keep it on an even keel. "I can see how you might take that position, but unfortunately your interpretation of the situation is, shall we say, highly questionable."

I watched the faces around me grow wide-eyed; I don't think they had ever seen someone stand up to a professor before. "When you hired us, it was made clear that not only didn't you believe in ghosts—your biggest concern was the students harming each other." I let that sink in. "You've set up a significant amount of equipment, none of which appears to be actually functional, even though it seems to have been funded by the University. You did not tell us that you were searching the house, nor what you were searching for. I'm of the opinion that you didn't tell the University what you were really doing, either. Which suggests to me that you may have misappropriated funds to privately benefit yourself and your students." I paused again, but not long enough to allow anyone to reply. "Yes, your son got hurt, but that was properly treated by us. As for the disappearance of Russell Quinton, the permanence of that situation and the long-term ramifications have yet to be determined."

"So, what if Quinton *has* vanished?" mumbled Loren. "What's one less lawyer? The world would be a damned sight better off with fewer of them."

"You're a pig, Fred," retorted Elaine. "A first-class pig."

"Sticks and stones, Elaine, sticks and stones."

"That's enough!" Megan barked. It wasn't a request; it was an order. "If we are going to get out of this, we need to start working together, or at least not working against each other." She paused and adopted a softer, more conciliatory tone. "That's going to mean some serious changes. First off, no one goes anywhere alone. We're an even number now, so were going to pair up at all times. And yes, that means sleeping arrangements as well. Second, we're going to repurpose some of this ghost hunting equipment. We need to see if anything has been picked up yet, and if so, exactly what."

"If Quinton moved about the house, the sensors could have picked him up," offered Delambre.

Megan pointed at the young man. "That's the kind of thinking we need. How long to review everything you've got?"

Delambre was hopeful, "With Plato's help, a couple hours. I could report in after lunch."

Hours later, Delambre reported back that things had not gone as well as expected.

"The cameras were tripped—in fact, all the cameras on the main floor were almost out of film. This is true of the second floor and lower part of the observatory as well. But nothing we set up in the lower floor caught anything of note."

"So, what did the cameras on the other floors capture?" The kid needed to be prompted.

Plato looked dejected. "I don't understand what happened—the images are all out of focus and cloudy." He handed me the stack of images. He was right. Each photograph seemed to have been corrupted in some manner or another. You could tell what room it was, and parts of the images were relatively unaffected, but in each a significant portion was nearly unidentifiable—terribly out of focus, blurry, or even warped or twisted into queer swirls. I handed them to Megan.

She flipped through them much more slowly than I had. "Well, this is interesting. She laid three images out next to each other. They were all images of the same room, taken in quick succession. "It isn't the film or the camera that's the problem. Whatever is triggering the sensor is almost invisible."

We all took a good look at what she had laid out. She was right—there was something there: a definitive shape moving through the room, caught three times, something large and oblong and outlined by the effect it was having on the camera.

"It's the same thing that we saw in the dining room," said Elaine. "A Kallikantzaroi."

Megan nodded. "These are the pictures from the second floor." She waved them in her hand. "Here's one of Quinton going into his room, and here's the rest of us." She tossed another set of photographs on the table. "And here's one of something barely visible going down the hall." She shuffled through the others. "And here's one where that same invisible thing appears to be standing outside of Quinton's room." She stared at it intensely and then reached into her pocket for a small jeweler's loupe. She examined the latest photograph and I saw her frown as she handed it to me.

The image was similar to all the others: there was a well-defined area that was distorted and swirled, but in this one there was something else. There in the madness of twisted color one could make out the eyes, nose and mouth—the face of Russell Quinton—and it was screaming.

Megan looked at me and I nodded. Then she turned back and pointed at Doctor Zorba, who had been looking over her shoulder at the images. "It's time we had a conversation about what is really going on here."

Doctor Socrates Zorba suddenly looked ashamed. As I glanced around the room, the entirety of the Miskatonic University Spiritualism Club seemed to share his guilt—even Elaine Zachirides. None of them spoke, and Dr. Zorba did not say anything either. We waited as the silence deepened and became more awkward, and it was not broken until Plato opened the door and announced that dinner was ready.

It took a few minutes for everyone to gain their composure. During that time, Plato and Cross finished setting the table and brought the food up from the kitchen. Frankly, I can't even remember what we had that night, but we ate it in uncomfortable silence. It was only after coffee had been served that civility was broken and Megan demanded answers. There were some nervous glances amongst the club members, and then, finally—and only after no one else seemed willing to share—the younger Zorba spoke up. "I'm assuming dad told you that Jackson Flux went a little crazy after his son died, started researching ways to contact the dead, and that he stole some University equipment to help in the effort."

I nodded. "That was the gist of it."

Delambre stepped in. "A few months back, I was tasked with cleaning out an old storeroom full of files. I found a whole box full of Flux's stuff. Notes, unpublished papers, notebooks full of calculations and one with what looked like designs for circuitry and something akin to a Faraday cage. It took me a few days to piece it all together and another week to check the calculations, but I think Flux was on to something."

"And what would that be?" Megan crossed her arms.

"To understand what Flux had been in the process of developing, you have to understand what he had been studying before his son had died." Delambre was becoming animated, moving his hands around on the counter. "Flux had been researching the motion and orbits of distant stellar objects—not moons or planets, but galaxies and galactic clusters. Before he went completely bonkers, he wrote a paper with Zwicky at

CalTech and Oort at Leiden University detailing the orbital relationships in the Coma Cluster—real genius stuff—not published until 1925, well after his disappearance. Anyway, he had made an observation—not an original one; apparently, Lord Kelvin, Henri Poincare and a Dutchman named Kapteyn had noticed similar phenomenon—when astronomers calculate the orbits of planets around the sun, the masses all seem to make sense, the math all works, when they do the calculations for larger objects in the universe—galaxies and the like—nothing works. The orbits and implied masses don't make sense."

Megan, who was smarter than I was, wasn't following. "What exactly does that mean?"

"Kelvin, Poincare and Kapteyn all concluded the same thing. The objects that we see in the sky, the light from stars and galaxies, what we think of as the universe, is only a small portion of what must exist out there. The rest of it is something else, something we can't see with our eyes or our telescopes. Something that doesn't generate or reflect back light, an entirely different kind of matter. Kelvin called it the *dark body*, Poincare used the term *materie obscure*, Zwicky's notes call it *dunkle Materie*—but it's all the same thing, what Flux called dark matter."

The younger Zorba suddenly, excitedly, stepped in. "This is where it gets strange," he added, and continued on. "Flux theorized that this extra-stellar dark matter was similar to what spiritualists called ectoplasm. His idea was that what we think of as ghosts are the dark matter remnants of human life forces, and that ectoplasm is dark matter shifting briefly into a different, more tangible state of matter—albeit unstable—which is why it can be only rarely photographed."

I looked at Megan and I saw her mouth the word "Dunwich." My eyes grew wide as I understood her meaning, and how this theory applied to Wilbur Whateley and his semi-visible sibling.

Plato Zorba wasn't stopping. "Flux's circuitry and Faraday cage may have been designed to capture ghosts, but for all practical purposes they should function to isolate and stabilize the underlying material that Flux thought ghosts were composed of—dark matter."

I was looking for the angle. "Which—would make you all very rich?"

It was Loren's turn to lead the discussion. "It's possible. A novel state of matter and energy source is worth exploring. Could you imagine owning the patent on petroleum or methane?"

I got it. I didn't like it, but I got it. "So why are we here? Flux leave out a calculation or two from his notes?"

Delambre sighed. "Something like that. His notes call for the Flux Cell —that's what we're calling it for now—to be tuned to the right harmonic frequency. To do that, he employed something called a resonator. We think that's what he stole the radio parts for."

The older Zorba must have seen my face. "What's wrong, Mister Peaslee?"

I closed my eyes and took a deep breath. "I've heard the term 'resonator' before." I wanted to say more, but Megan shook her head in a subtle— almost imperceptible—way, so I shut my mouth.

She redirected the conversation. "So, what do you expect to find here? Plans for the resonator, or notes towards its design?"

"Finding the plans would suit us just fine," chimed in Doctor Zorba. "But Flux's financials show that he bought several rolls of copper wire the month before his death. There are also a few receipts for various electronic components. We think that Flux may have actually built a prototype of the resonator, maybe even a Flux Cell. If we can find that, our mission would be complete."

"Do you have any idea how big the resonator is?"

"That's the problem, Mister Peaslee," replied Delambre. "Given the designs I've seen for the components it is supposed to interface with, it could be relatively small. Perhaps no bigger than a book."

"Which means it could be anywhere," suggested Loren. "Our plan was to go through each of the rooms meticulously."

"While distracting us with a fake ghost hunt," said Megan, I saw that she was noticeably perturbed.

"Which didn't turn out so well," sighed Doctor Zorba. "I never expected to have to deal with a real ghost."

I challenged that notion. "I don't think we're dealing with a ghost."

Plato Zorba was flabbergasted, "Then what exactly do you think that thing we saw was, if it wasn't a ghost?"

Megan took over. "In reviewing various documents made available to us for security purposes, we have become aware of several incidents that seem tangentially related to our current situation. These include the so-called Dunwich Horror, the Tillinghast murders, and the disappearance of Henry Wentworth Akeley. All of these events have reportedly involved the manifestations of entities that were only partially visible." A small murmur of disbelief went through the students. "The witnesses were reliable, and several are faculty at Miskatonic University." She said this to quell the mumbling, but instead it seemed to generate even more. "In fact, both my husband and I have seen several similar entities."

I nodded as everybody turned in my direction. "We don't know exactly what this thing is, but I assure you it isn't the lingering spirit of a deceased human being."

Delambre seemed less skeptical than the others, "You said you don't know exactly what this thing is—that implies you have an idea."

"When Wilbur Whateley was killed by the guard dog in the University library, his normally hidden nether regions bore some similarities to that of an octopus, a crocodile, an elephant, and insects. Photographs of the body failed to develop, much in the manner of what we saw with Plato's attempts here. The body itself decayed rapidly, dissolving, almost sub-limating in a matter of hours. Both of these facts suggest that Whateley was not wholly made of normal terrestrial matter."

After pausing for more murmuring from the group, I continued: "This is very similar to events reported by Professor Wilmarth in which a man named Henry Wentworth Akeley not only encountered what he described as extraterrestrial creatures, but also admitted killing one and capturing the body." Another murmur. "As with Whateley, the pictures Akeley took showed nothing, and the body dissolved in a matter of hours, providing no trace evidence whatsoever."

Delambre was suddenly excited. "Have you ever heard about the Arkham Meteorite?" he asked. Seeing that we hadn't, he continued. "Flux was obsessed with the thing. Back in 1882, a meteorite fell on a farm west of town. Researchers from the University went and recovered several fragments. Everything they recovered dissolved away in the same manner as you've described. Flux was convinced that the meteorite was made out of dark matter."

Megan smiled. "I think what we are saying here is that Professor Flux may have failed to contact the spirit of his dead son, but instead somehow brought a dark matter entity here—to Earth—where it has for some reason remained. The thing trapped in this house isn't a ghost, but something extraterrene, and it's responsible for the disappearance of both Flux and Quinton."

"You're saying that Flux captured one of H. G. Wells' Martians and it's running around killing people?" muttered Cross. "Do you have any idea how insane that sounds?"

"Actually," interjected Delambre, "what she is saying is actually worse. Wells' Martians were flesh and blood, they followed known and understandable laws of physics and biology. What Misses Peaslee is describing is something very different—something that is made of substances that follow physical laws we don't understand."

"How is that possible?" asked Cross. "The laws of physics and chemistry are universal."

Delambre shook his head. "Maybe not. Think of our universe as a soap bubble, and everything that we can see—the planets, the sun, the other stars, other galaxies, even nebulae are pinned to the surface of that bubble. The laws that govern the behavior of objects on the bubble would be very different than those that operated within the bubble." Delambre paused to let that sink in. "If objects from the bubble's interior were to intrude into the space occupied by the surface, the results for the local residents might be catastrophic—monstrous, even."

Elaine seemed to grasp what Delambre was trying to explain, "You mean we might see these things, these dark matter objects, as monsters."

"From a purely subjective point of view, yes—we might see these things and because they behave in ways we don't understand, and are capable of moving in ways we aren't, we might call them monsters, or demons, or even ghosts. But objectively . . ." He paused, obviously regretting his train of thought.

"Go on," urged Megan.

"This is what Flux and his colleagues figured out by studying the nature of how things moved in the universe. Their calculations suggest that the vast majority of mass in the universe isn't what we can see, but rather the dark matter that we can't see. This means that the universe is mostly dark matter, which means objectively, if there are dark matter entities, this is *their* universe, not ours. They aren't the aberrations—the monsters or ghosts . . . *we* are."

The older Zorba took a large gulp from his drink and set the glass down on the table. "Well, that's a sobering thought. He looked around the table and focused on myself and Megan, "How do we protect ourselves from something like what you're describing?"

"I'm not sure," I confessed. "In the Tillinghast case, a resonator was used to stimulate the pineal gland so that those affected could see these things. In Dunwich, Doctor Armitage used a powder he concocted based on a formula he found in an ancient spell book."

"Could we build a resonator?" Plato asked.

"In theory," said Delambre, "but in practice we would need to be able to tune it to the right frequency; that might take months. But remember, Flux was already in the process of designing and building one. It might already exist. All we have to do is find it."

Megan's hand darted out and picked up the photos again. "You've captured the thing with cameras on both the main floor and the floor with the bedrooms, but not down in the kitchen, or the basement."

"So why not in these places?" mused Cross. "What makes them different?"

Megan looked at me and I at her. "The metallic inlay," we said in unison.

"What metallic inlay?" asked Cross.

"It's in the walls and floors and windows," I said.

Delambre pushed his chair out and dropped to the floor to inspect the alloy he found in the design there. "I think this is mu-metal." he looked up and realized nobody knew what he was talking about. "It's a nickel-iron-copper alloy that is used to shield against magnetic fields." His eyes met mine, "You say this is all through the house?"

I nodded.

He stood up and brushed himself off. "I think we now know more than we did a few minutes ago."

"I think you might be right," Megan agreed.

"What are you two talking about?" demanded Loren, he seemed frustrated with the conversation so far.

"We don't need to look for the Flux Cell anymore—we've found it."

Loren wasn't catching on. "Where? Here in this room?"

Delambre was smiling and shaking his head triumphantly. "Not the room, Fred—*the house*. Flux built his dark matter holding cell out of the entire house."

"Well, not the entire house," I corrected him. "Just two floors, the wooden ones, he could inlay the—what did you call it?—mu-metal, and in the observatory where he has hung similar netting."

"Yes, and if what you say is true, this thing—this Kallikantzaros—is probably trapped inside the cell, inside the house, or at least part of it."

"Then why can't we see it, or at least the distortion it makes?" The question from the elder Zorba was more a demand than an inquiry.

"It only comes out at night," suggested Elaine. "Perhaps the sunlight interacts with the dark matter and suppresses it somehow, or maybe the light magnifies the effect of the Flux Cell."

Megan had grown quiet and her eyes had developed a faraway look that told me she was deep in thought. "If the creature is trapped somewhere inside the house, then maybe Quinton is in the same place."

There was a general murmur of hopeful agreement that was suddenly shattered by Elaine standing up in stark terror. "If Quinton could still be alive, then so could my father—trapped for years with whatever it was he brought down from out there! We have to help him!" Her voice had risen to a shrill, panicked tone. Plato immediately went to her.

"We really need to find Flux's notes, figure out what he did and how he did it—and maybe how to undo it," said Megan. "Where haven't you looked yet?"

It was Loren who spoke up first. "The observatory—we haven't even touched the observatory."

"But you were in the observatory on the first day," countered Elaine, "I saw you myself."

He was immediately on the defensive. "You are sadly mistaken."

"No, I'm sure of it, I saw you go in." Elaine said, and the tone of her voice was adamant.

Loren did not seem to enjoy being challenged. With indignation filling his face, he pushed back his chair, stood up from the table and muttered, "I'm not going to sit here and be called a liar." He waved at Elaine dismissively and stalked out of the room, almost stomping his boots as he walked up the steps.

"But he was there," she insisted. "Why would he lie?"

"Why does Fred do anything?" asked Plato, his hands went to Elaine's shoulders as he continued to try to calm her.

The peace of the room was suddenly broken by a sudden thump from something large hitting the floor upstairs. There was a horrible sound—one that I didn't think could be made by a human throat. It started as a human scream, one that was recognizable as belonging to Loren, but then it transformed into a warbling tone that slowly faded into the distance, leaving only a faint echo reverberating through the house.

We ran upstairs as fast as we could, but we found nothing. Loren, like Quinton, was gone—snatched away by a preternatural hunter of inter-dimensional origin and taken somewhere we couldn't even begin to understand.

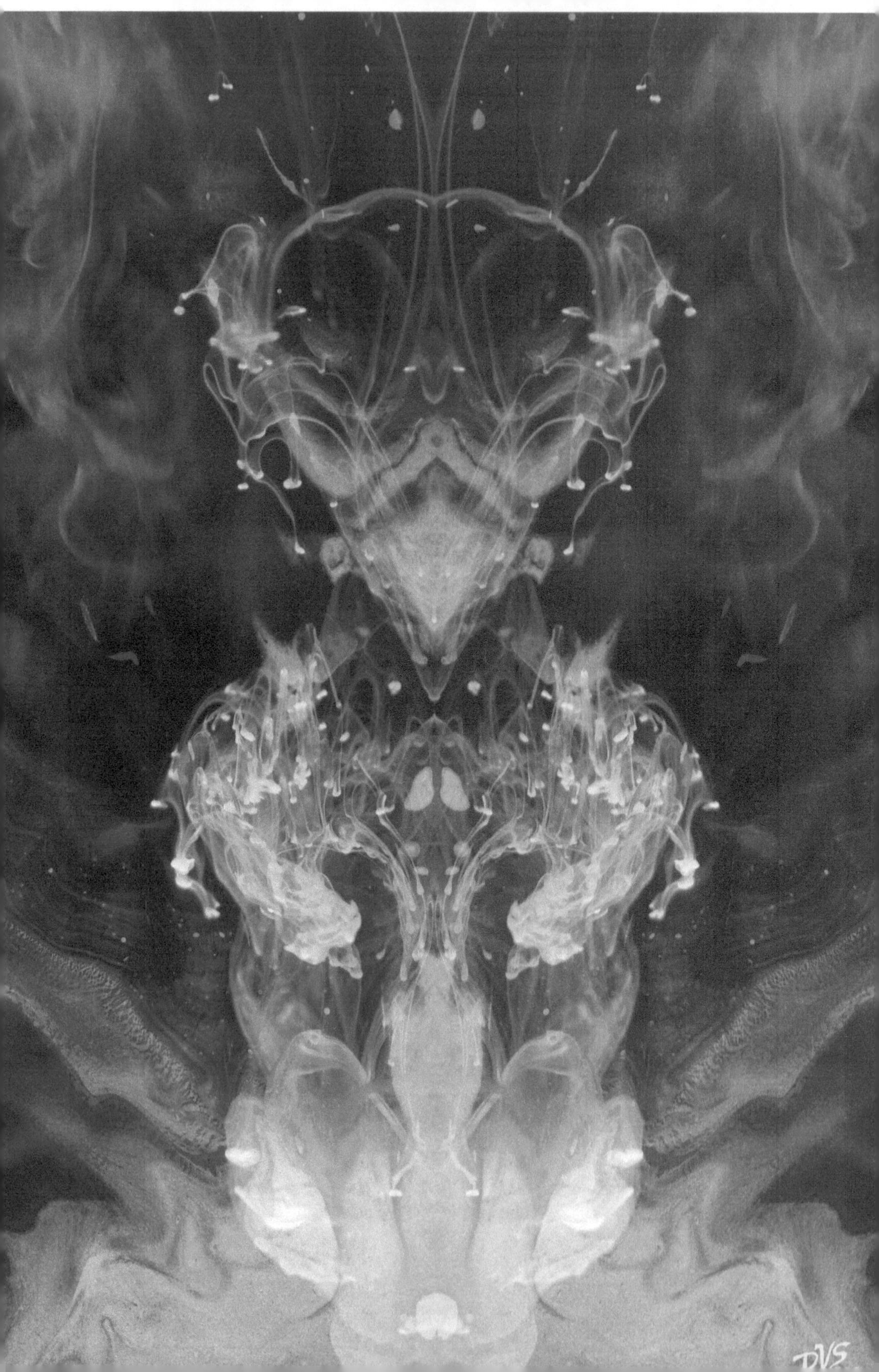

December 27, 1928

We spent the night in the kitchen, on the floor, with the oven on to supply some semblance of heat. After we had lost Loren, no one wanted to go hunting around in the house—not even as a group—so we retired to the kitchen, using it as a kind of safe room. The irony of the situation had not escaped us. There was nothing special about the kitchen; quite the contrary. It was the rest of the house that was special—that had been turned into a cage for something from *out there*. A thing that—if we understood the situation properly—had been imprisoned for years.

I thought it a horrible condition, to be a prisoner for all those years, but then I wondered if it even understood what had happened to it, and whether it was even capable of such understanding. It could have been like a goldfish in a bowl, too stupid to even know it was detained. And then I started thinking about what Delambre had said, that the physical rules of the universe might be different for it, and I wondered if time passed in the same manner for it as it did for us, or if it even had a concept of time.

Professor Zorba made breakfast—Greek omelets with spiced potatoes. We ate in silence, devouring our portions, happy to have something warm in our bellies after the long, cold night. As we sat there in the afterglow of the meal, sipping *kahvesi*—thick black Turkish coffee—we watched as the flames that warmed the pot began to flicker. At first, we thought it was the wind—that the flame caught in some subtle and undetected breeze. For a brief moment we thought perhaps it was the invisible thing that somehow had escaped its bounds and was attacking the necessities that sustained us. But then the flames grew small and weak and then finally went out completely, and we knew the truth. The gas supply that we had estimated sufficient for our stay had been used up overnight. We were now going to be forced back into the rest of the house where we could use the fireplaces to keep warm, and where the thing could reach us as well. But at least it was daylight, and—while daylight was not a guarantee that we would be safe—we felt as if we had time to figure out what we were going to do. After some minor discussion, we wandered upstairs and started a fire in the main hall. Through the windows we could see that it had begun snowing again. As the fire started to warm the room, most of our group wandered to the window to look out at the wintery scene in all its starkly beautiful New England glory.

Elaine Zachirides sighed as she surveyed the landscape beyond the window. Then she recited a bit of poetry:

> "Unwarmed by any sunset light
> The gray day darkened into night,
> A night made hoary with the swarm,
> And whirl-dance of the blinding storm,
> As zigzag, wavering to and fro,
> Crossed and recrossed the winged snow
> And ere the early bedtime came
> The white drift piled the window-frame,
> And through the glass the clothes-line posts
> Looked in like tall and sheeted ghosts"

Cross chuckled, "I'm not sure Whittier is appropriate at the moment."

"I think it's rather indicative of the situation," countered Megan. "After all, we're just as snowbound as Whittier's characters, though perhaps not as congenial."

Elaine looked at Megan, "We used to be. After all we even had shirts made up. Hand-embroidered with a planchette over the breast pocket and Miskatonic University Spiritualism Club on the back. We used to wear them to meetings and then go down together to the Student Union for cake and coffee afterwards."

"What happened?" asked Megan.

"Hmm?"

"You spoke in the past tense. You used to do those things, so what happened?"

A puzzled look came across Elaine's face. "I'm not sure; I never really thought about it before." But you could tell that she was thinking about it now. "Maybe it had something to do with our trip out to Dunwich back in November."

"You went out to Dunwich, after what happened there?"

The young student nodded. "Lots of students did, we kind of helped in the relief effort. Helped salvage what we could from collapsed houses. Helped rebuild houses and barns. Ran kitchens. Taught classes. The medical students opened up a field hospital. The Club tried to gather what documentation we could concerning local ghost lore and legends. There was a book published back around Nineteen Hundred and Ten, *The Spectral Wood*. It detailed hauntings in the area around Dean's Corners, Aylesbury and Dunwich. Doctor Zorba got in our heads that we should see how the stories had changed over the last twenty years, with the goal of producing updated versions."

"Sounds interesting."

"You would have thought so," agreed Elaine, "but it wasn't. Some of the families, houses and locations that had been documented in the book were gone—some lost through time and development, a few leveled by the Horror. This we expected, but what we didn't expect was the complete loss of local color—maybe loss isn't the right word. All the old stories about haunted houses, woods and graveyards had been supplanted by tales of the Whateleys. Even in Aylesbury, which is a fair distance from Dunwich, all local tales had been effectively eliminated. People still knew that a place had once been haunted, they could still remember that there had been stories about such places, but the legends had stagnated. The old tales hadn't been added to or modified at all. And there weren't any new ones either. All the old tales had been overshadowed by tales of Wizard

Whateley, his daughter Lavinia and his grandson Wilbur. It was so bad that Doctor Zorba suggested that, from a sociological point of view, it was as if the region had been so focused on the Whateleys that the tales about the Whateley family had somehow supplanted all the other stories in the region, purging the place of any other source of phantasmal lore. Cross had another more colorful way of putting it. He said 'There are no ghosts in Dunwich Country; the Whateleys have gone and eaten them all.' Isn't that a funny thing to say?"

Megan nodded, but I blanched at the thought that Cross might have inadvertently hit on a grain of truth. I was grateful when Delambre came in and suggested that he might have found a way to keep us safe inside the house.

"We can use the wire mesh that is draped around the inside of the observatory. It's made of the same mu-metal as the inlay. We can hang it in here like a tent. If it's really acting as a Flux Cell and keeping this thing imprisoned, then we should be able to build another cage and keep ourselves protected."

I smiled, "That is a great idea, but I have a slightly better one." I pulled him aside and very quietly explained how to build on his idea and make it significantly better. When I had finished, he just stared at me for a moment and then ran off back to the observatory.

Megan gave me a puzzled look but I just waved her away. "I'm heading up to search Loren's room. I shouldn't be long."

"Why would you search Loren's room?"

"Before he was taken, Elaine said that she had seen Loren in the observatory. Loren denied this, vehemently. But I think she was right, and I think he may have found something we desperately need right now."

"Scream if you get attacked."

"Screaming isn't going to get you there fast enough to help me."

My wife nodded. "I know, but at least I'll know what happened to you."

I marched off without another word.

Frederick Loren's room was as I expected. At every turn, there were symbols that confirmed his life of wealth and privilege, and the manner in which they were treated indicated his lack of respect for their cost and their craftsmanship. On the bureau there was a toiletry kit—leather, with silver adornments—but the latch had been forced open and a bottle of cologne had at one point been broken inside of it. There were matching horsehair brushes with carved horn handles, but the bristles had been crushed through misuse and improper storage. By all rights, this was a set that should have lasted a gentleman a lifetime or more—but he had destroyed it in a matter of years. The same could be said of his luggage, and the hand-tailored clothing that had been thrown haphazardly inside. The bed was unmade, and there were dishes on the nightstand. A half-empty bottle of liquor sat on the floor; the distinctive label identified it as Open Grave Whisky, a bootlegged brand that wasn't the worst option on the black market, but it wasn't the best, either. It was, perhaps, most notorious for the rumor that it was distilled in an abandoned cemetery somewhere outside New Orleans.

Loren's luggage sat to one side of the room. Two suitcases were open, and it was obvious that he hadn't bothered to unpack, and was living out of his bags. A third suitcase was an Osilite trunk manufactured by H. J. Cave of Great Britain. It was a prestigious brand, but once again the owner had treated it like a dog that needed an occasional beating to make sure it remained submissive. A manual examination of the lock confirmed that it was engaged. It took a few minutes, and more effort than I expected, to force the latch open—enough so that my opinion of the manufacturer increased substantially, and I made a mental note to look into ordering one for Megan.

Inside were more clothes—how many shirts did the man need?— including a few sweaters, a pair of fur-lined hiking boots and a matching pair of gloves. It was all rather pedestrian; the hidden compartment was only half shut, and even a fledgling customs agent would have noticed it. Inside was a small wooden crate with a stamp on the outside that said "Bose Inverse Coherer Mark IV." I opened up the box and was unsurprised to find a small metallic casing, about the size of my hand, with a thick glass front. Inside were numerous wires and diodes that had been strung together to form a crude Y. On the top and the bottom, where the three terminals met the casing, were connecting ports where electrical connections could be made. The object was surprisingly light, and while I didn't recognize anything about it, I suspected that it was likely the long sought-after resonator. Loren had clearly discovered it in the observatory and secreted it away for his own personal gain. Now we had not only the Flux Cell but also the resonator, and all we had to do was figure out how they worked together. That was something that I would leave for Mr. Delambre.

I found him where I expected to: in the observatory, working on some of the extra metallic netting. I waved the small metal box at him like a bone in front of a dog. He dropped what he was doing, ran over and snatched it from my hands. He turned it over and over, fascinated by the thing he held, as if it were something precious—something ancient and astounding.

"These look like electrical input points," he said, pointing at the two ports at the top, "and this should be where the Flux Cell is connected." He turned it over again. "There isn't a voltage controller, but that isn't a problem. I saw one here somewhere." He wandered over toward the workbench.

"If this is the resonator you were looking for, why isn't it attached to the Flux Cell? And how is the cell still actively imprisoning our ghost without any power?"

Delambre nodded, "The cell probably functions similarly to an electret, a material that is similar to a magnet in that it generates an external electric field. The resonator is probably used to essentially tune that field but isn't needed to maintain it."

"So, you don't need the resonator to power the netting?"

"Since this netting wasn't connected to the rest it probably needs to be properly tuned. Once that is done, we shouldn't need the resonator, but having all the components connected might have other uses."

"Such as?"

"Well, I've been thinking. We know that the Flux Cell functions as a cage, but why? My first thought was that it functioned as a physical barrier that the ghost can't get through, like a wall or prison bars. But the other possibility is that it functions similarly to the *Grenzhochspannungshindernis*, the so-called Wire of Death that the Germans deployed along the border between Belgium and the Netherlands. It was a simple barbed wire fence electrified with two thousand volts. If this second scenario is the case, then, in theory, we could use the resonator to change the Flux Cell—using it to herd the ghost in the direction we want, controlling it, perhaps even killing it if we had to."

I closed my eyes and sighed. "I would prefer not to have to go down that path. This creature—Elaine called it a *Kallikantzaros*—it didn't come

          THE MISKATONIC UNIVERSITY SPIRITUALISM CLUB

here by choice. Flux likely brought it here by accident, and it has been trapped here against its will. That it has become aggressive toward humans is a completely understandable response. If we can find a way to release it, we should do so as soon as possible."

"We could do that now, just by tearing down some of the netting or ripping up the inlay," suggested Delambre.

"If we did that, we might lose Quinton and Loren."

Delambre was initially incredulous at my suggestion. "We've already lost . . ." but then he saw my meaning. "I hadn't thought of that. They might not be dead, just trapped within the Kallikantzaros, like Jonah and the whale."

"And if we figure out how this technology works, we just might be able to get this thing to cough them back up."

It was then that the relative quiet was pierced by a shrieking scream that reverberated through the halls and walls of the house. I could tell by the pitch that it was a woman's scream, but it wasn't Megan—though I hadn't often heard her scream. Reflexively, I bolted from the observatory, my hand fumbling under my coat to free my gun. Delambre was right on my tail. I pushed through the door to the lounge and past a wide-eyed and bewildered Cross. Why in the Hell was Cross by himself? Hadn't we told them to stick together? From the hallway I could hear Elaine sobbing in the main hall. As we closed the distance, Megan came up beside me carrying her own gun, though to be honest I wasn't sure what exactly we were going to shoot at, or what good it would do.

Elaine Zachirides was in the Main Hall, her back against the wall, her hands clinging to the wood as if she was trying to anchor herself to it. Her eyes were wide and wild, her mouth open and her lips drawn back in terror. There were noises coming from her, but they weren't words. On the floor there was a jumble of wood and a trail of slushy boot prints, but they didn't belong to Elaine.

Megan and I scanned the room, and once we knew who was where I nodded to her and she crossed over to Elaine's side. "Elaine, it's okay— whatever it was is gone. It's gone. It's gone and you're still here. Are you hurt?"

Elaine shook her head and blubbered "Nnnnooo."

That's when Doctor Zorba did his own head count. "Where's Plato?"

he blurted out with concern.

Elaine tried again to disappear into the wall and said nothing while failing to do so. Megan tried to comfort her but Elaine fell to her knees and lowered her head and sobbed.

Suddenly Socrates Zorba was no longer an academic—he was a father. He was on his knees and his hands were on Elaine's shoulders. "Where is my son?" he yelled.

She looked up and her eyes were filled with madness. "It, it , it . . . "

The elder Zorba was infuriated in his panic. "Tell me, you stupid girl!"

Suddenly laughing like a maniac, Elaine grabbed her mentor by the lapels of his shirt and looked him directly in the eyes. "It ate him. It came out of the air and it ate him! Swallowed him all up in one bite. Like he was a piece of popcorn." This idea seemed to amuse her. "Didn't even bother to chew!" She fell back against the wall, giggling in madness while Doctor Socrates Zorba collapsed to the floor in shock.

I turned to Delambre. "Take Cross and get back to the observatory. I want that Flux Cell up and running as soon as possible!" They didn't say a word in protest—they just scurried back to work on the thing that still might be able to save us all. It was only after they were gone that I remembered that my gun was in my hand and that I was waving it about as if I was mad. As I put the piece of cold steel back in its holster, I couldn't help but think that perhaps a little madness was what we needed if we were going to get out of this mess.

By dinner the netting was up. We had decided to make our stand in the main hall, as it provided quick access to both the kitchen and the front door in case we needed to evacuate. The room looked like something out of the *Arabian Nights,* for the ceiling was now draped with large pieces of the wire mesh netting, all wired up to a crude control panel that allowed Delambre to not only release the nets, but also to direct and regulate the voltage as it coursed through the resonator. It was a decent plan, but one fraught with danger. It would take time to find the right voltage to make the netting work, meaning the Kallikantzaros would be free to act. Additionally, the electrical charge coursing through the netting presented a significant risk to the rest of us. A quick shock might knock us on our butts, but if one of us were trapped underneath, the sustained effect, although brief, might be deadly. It was a calculated risk that both Megan and I were willing to take. We had no choice but to proceed, though, so we did what we could to make sure that everybody else knew the inherent danger. Only Delambre had any sort of protective gear—he wore a pair of insulated electrical gloves in case he had to repair any connections. We had thought about giving them to someone else, but he was the only person qualified to operate the equipment and to make any rushed repairs. Delambre and the elder Zorba were going over the plan a third time when I left them to find Megan.

As I said, it was a decent plan. But I also knew that even the best-laid plans often went astray. Which is why we were all prepared to run out into the snow and brave the overnight temperatures in the hopes that Dudley would arrive in the morning to find us before we froze to death. I just hoped it wouldn't come to that.

Megan was sitting in the corner of the room, alone for the first time in hours. She had done her best to keep Elaine calm, and when talking hadn't worked she had finally given up and slipped a sedative into Elaine's tea; Elaine was now sleeping soundly in the corner. Megan looked more frustrated than satisfied. Like all of us, she was tired of waiting, tired of not being able to do anything—tired of feeling useless.

I sidled up next to her and put my arm around her shoulder. "Having a good holiday?"

She wrinkled her nose. "You take me to the nicest places."

I chuckled. "Nice people though."

"What's left of them." She scanned the room. "Three down, four to go."

"You're not including us in the head count?"

She shrugged. "We can leave anytime we want. This idea that the snow and cold is keeping us in here—that might work for the clients, but you and I both know that we could walk out that door and be perfectly fine."

"You mean because I'm . . ."

"Complicated." She took my hand in hers and patted it. "We're both complicated—very, *very* complicated."

I closed my eyes and put my head down on her shoulder. "A good word that, 'complicated.' Covers all manner of sins."

I felt her hand stroke my hair. "Is that what you think we are—sins?"

"Monsters are a kind of sin, aren't they?"

"You aren't a monster Robert," she grabbed me softly by the cheeks and kissed my forehead. "You're a man. A little cold, somewhat stiff, and you don't sleep, but you're a man through and through." She kissed me again. "In fact, you remind me a lot of my father. Now there was a man."

I glared at her through half opened eyes. "Are you talking about before or after he died?"

"Does it matter?"

I shrugged. "Not really," and then I pulled her into the crook of my arm and let her fall asleep.

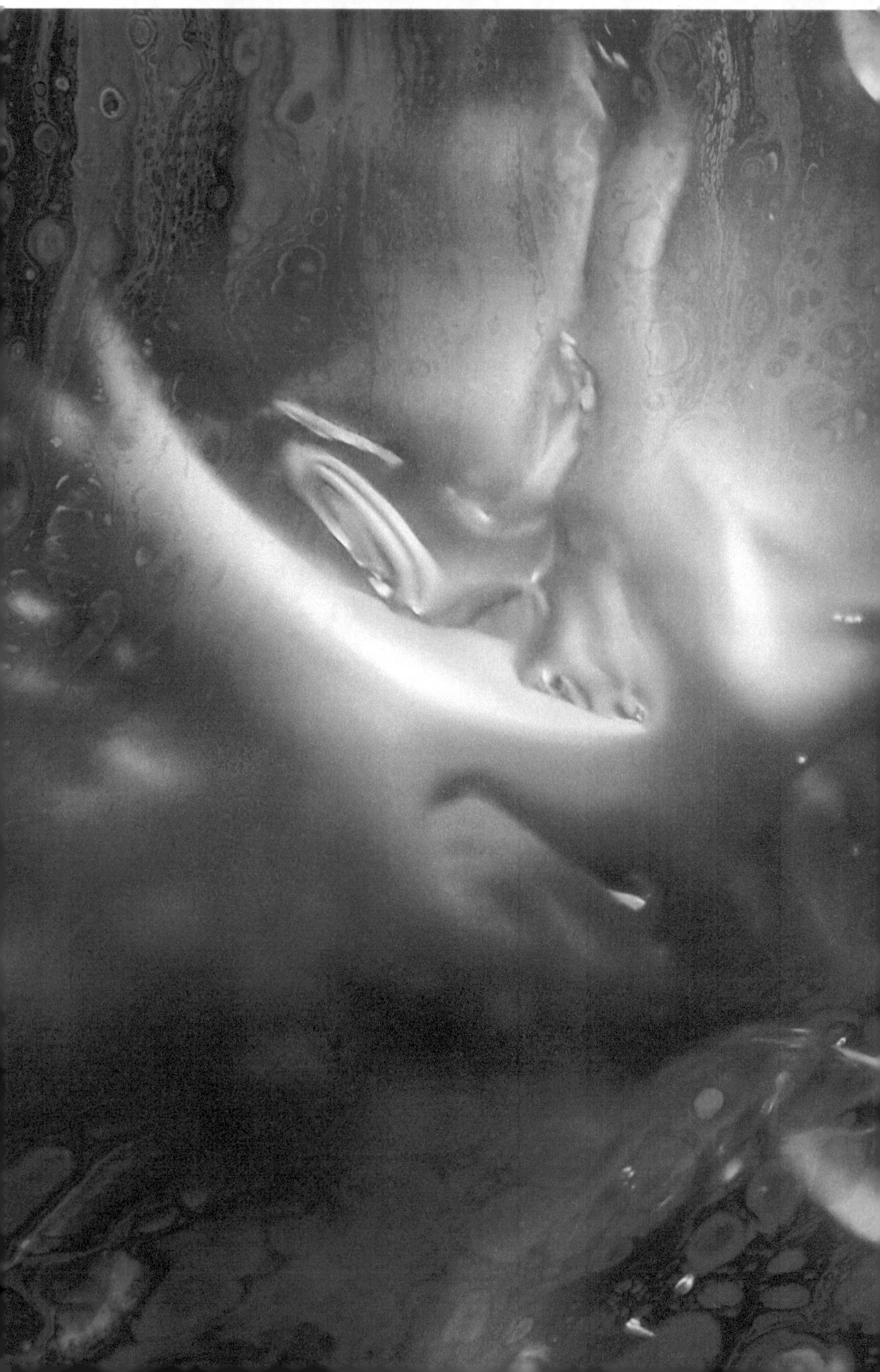

DECEMBER 28, 1928
— EVENING —

The attack came in the wee hours of the morning—that strange and uncomfortable time way past midnight, when the previous day is well and truly over, and yet the next day has not really begun. The opposite of twilight, it is a time when the world feels pregnant with potential. It is a time unknown to many, a time when most are happily ensconced in their beds, wrapped up in blankets and bed sheets, their eyes closed tight, their heads filled with what fancies they could muster to erase the dullness of the previous day and the impending dullness of the day ahead. Most, but not all. Some, like myself, are up during these hours, waiting and watching. We see things. We see lots of things. Lots and lots of things. And sometimes we hear things.

Particularly when nothing else is moving.

The first sign that something was happening was small, nearly insignificant, and I almost didn't notice it. It was a slight fluttering noise, almost imperceptible. It rapidly became clearer and more defined until it sounded to my ears like the flapping of many bird wings, as if a flock of pigeons had just taken flight before me. It wasn't a fearful sound—not terrifying or horrific, it was just a sound, a sound like any other. It unnerved me nonetheless, and grabbed my attention, for despite its utter ordinariness it was a sound that should not have been there. For, after all, there was nothing there to make that sound, nothing at all—nothing on Earth. But this thing wasn't from Earth.

With the fluttering noise it came, dragging itself into existence. It was an inhuman, unearthly thing the size of a small man or a large dog. It was—in general form—an oval with armored plates, and in this it bore some semblance to a pill bug, but there were on its underside a myriad of claws both large and small, simple and complex, which reminded me vaguely of a crab or lobster. From the dorsal plates on its back rose a cluster of thick jointed spines that seemed to swim through the very air. It was from these that the fluttering sound was coming, with each stroke it pulled itself into being, becoming more and more visible, more solid, more real. As it came, the noise grew louder, and the frequency changed. In moments it went from a fluttering to a dull flapping and then a vicious unbridled buzzing that hurt my ears and made my teeth ache.

The sound stirred the others—all except Elaine, who was still drugged. I put my arm across Megan's chest to keep her still, to keep her from waking up guns blazing. She still reached for her guns, but much more slowly, more deliberately than she would have otherwise. "What the fuck are we waiting for?"

"It's not in position yet," I said as I glanced over at Delambre. He was watching the thing as it slid through the air effortlessly, like a duck on the surface of a lake. It was almost where we wanted it—almost there. "Just a few feet more."

We watched silently as it moved ever closer to the spot we needed it to reach—closer, and closer, and the tension in those seconds became unbearable. I was startled when the room filled with a screeching sound as Elaine woke up, screaming *"Kallikantzaroi!"* and the plan started to go pear-shaped.

The thing turned toward Elaine—toward the noise, toward the shrieking Greek—and it did the most unexpected thing: it screamed back. It was a terrifying noise, like the wind howling through a thousand metal pipes, and something else—something like a human voice or voices screaming out in terror but layered on top of each other in almost a perfect harmony of fear and terror. There was a mouth of sorts embedded beneath something that could have been a head or a mushroom or perhaps even a kind of convoluted coral. It swam smoothly through the air toward Elaine, snarling and gnashing whatever it had that passed for teeth.

Elaine screamed. Delambre panicked. He pulled one of several pins out and released the rope that held one of the nets in place. It sped up along the wall and through the rafters, and halfway across the room a net fell and ensnared our prey. It didn't seem to notice, or if it did it didn't seem to care. The netting just draped over it like a silk sheet, obscuring some features and enhancing others. Covered like that, the dorsal spines became like wings and the whole thing looked like some sort of angel, straight out of the Old Testament, something beautiful and terrible and monstrous all at the same time. Across the room I saw Richard Cross—the rational psychiatry student—fall to his knees and begin to pray.

"Tuning the current," Delambre yelled, and I caught a whiff of ozone as the netting began to softly glow. But the creature didn't react. Instead, it just kept crawling through the air toward Elaine, forcing her to scramble away. Delambre yelled again; I couldn't make out what he said, but I knew he was adjusting the frequency.

This time the thing—the Kallikantzaroi—reacted. It fell to the floor, clearly writhing in agony as the netting closed in around it. I caught a glimpse of a figure at the controls manipulating the voltage and frequency, but it wasn't Delambre. Delambre was against the wall nursing his jaw. At the controls was Doctor Zorba, clearly reveling in the power he suddenly had.

"You took my son from me, you monster!" He shouted. "I'm going to make sure you pay!"

I went for Zorba, meaning to stop him from torturing the entity, but Megan grabbed my arm. "Robert, look at it! Look at what is happening!"

I turned my attention back to the creature writhing on the floor, but where once there had been just one creature there was now something else. The netting was cutting through the Kallikantzaroi—it was being dissected, subdivided not into two parts, not three, but five parts. One was clearly just a smaller version of the Kallikantzaroi, but the other four were more familiar, more terrestrial forms. They were clearly human, and clearly in just as much agony as the Kallikantzaroi.

I crossed the room in a leap and a bound and easily pushed Zorba away from the control box. I grabbed Delambre and pulled him back to where he could control things. I forced him to look at what was happening just a few yards away. Quinton, Loren and the younger Zorba were almost free—you could almost make out their features—and there was another man, one that I didn't recognize, but who could only be the missing Doctor Flux!

The netting was doing exactly what we had hoped it would, but there was an unintended side-effect. Most of its material mass gone, the Kallikantzaroi was significantly smaller now, and it had somehow managed to squirm out from underneath the netting. Even now at only a fraction of its size it still appeared as something to fear—something that, if it wanted to, could cause a significant amount of damage. I turned to Delambre and told him to drop a second net. He did so without hesitation, and once again the creature was draped in the netting of a Flux Cell. Delambre didn't need to be told to switch the power—he flipped the switch immediately—although at a much lower frequency. In an instant the Kallikantzaroi was our prisoner, and the students and one other were back in the real world.

"Now that we have it," said Delambre, "what do we do with it?"

I didn't bother to answer. I just grabbed the gloves and took off for the creature's side, donning the protective gear as I ran. I had had an idea, and I had little time to discuss it, and even less desire to. Above the roaring and screeching and Megan telling me to stop I grabbed one edge of the electrified netting and pulled it off of the Kallikantzaroi, freeing it from our trap. But I didn't stop there—in a fluid motion, I flung the empowered cell through the air and into the wall.

I could hear Delambre over everybody else trying to stop me. "The whole system will depolarize!" he shouted as he dove behind the couch. He hadn't understood that that was exactly what I was hoping to accomplish. I was expecting more of a light show—an explosion, perhaps some fireworks or arcing electrical bolts—but there was actually very little to see. The netting hit the wall, and it established a connection with the inlay. There was a flash of blue light as the circuitry that had been embedded throughout the house changed its charge, and then things went quiet. Very quiet. Dead quiet.

We all stood there in the quiet, in the stillness. Heads turned and our eyes darted about as we sought our adversary, but the room was empty—the thing had vanished completely.

"Is it gone?" ventured Cross meekly.

I almost said yes, but then the hairs on the back of my neck stood up and heard that terrible fluttering sound, and I watched as the Kallikantzaroi clawed its way back into view. It was different this time—there was an elegance to it. When I'd first seen it, it had been armored and beetle-like; it was now lithe, sleek and delicate. Where once its dorsal spikes had clawed through the air, they now had vast sail-like wings that kept it suspended gracefully in the ether. The fat fungal blob I'd surmised was its head was now covered in clusters of multicolored strands that writhed and twisted and contrived themselves into a complex—almost recursive—geometric design that made my eyes hurt when I looked at it. It was still terrifying, but there was something graceful about it now, something primal and oddly benevolent.

It floated there, serene and delicate, and somehow I knew that it was examining us, evaluating what we were and what we had done. It raised a single multi-clawed appendage as if in salute and then rose through the ceiling along a vector that was not up or down or left or right, but some entirely other direction that I have no words for, and yet I could still follow it as it flew out of the confines of that house and into the weird space from which it had originally been drawn.

Nearby, Doctor Zorba was covering his son with a blanket while Cross and Delambre did the same for Loren and Quinton. All seemed quite well, if a little nude, and perhaps in shock.

Megan was covering the shivering form of the fourth person. "Professor Flux," she smiled as she tried to force his hair back into a semblance of normalcy. "Let's get you cleaned up a little bit here."

He looked around the main hall and quickly assessed the damage. "Young lady, I'm not exactly sure that my appearance is a priority."

She giggled just a bit. "You've been gone a long time, Professor, but first impressions are still important." She spun him around carefully and whispered in his ear. "Professor Flux, may I introduce you to your daughter?"

The old man gave my wife a confused glance and then stared at the young woman who was slowly walking toward him. "Elaine?" There was a flash of recognition in his eyes. "Elaine, oh—you look so much like your mother!"

Elaine closed the gap and threw her arms around him "Daddy!"

It took a moment, but Megan finally made her way over to me. I looked

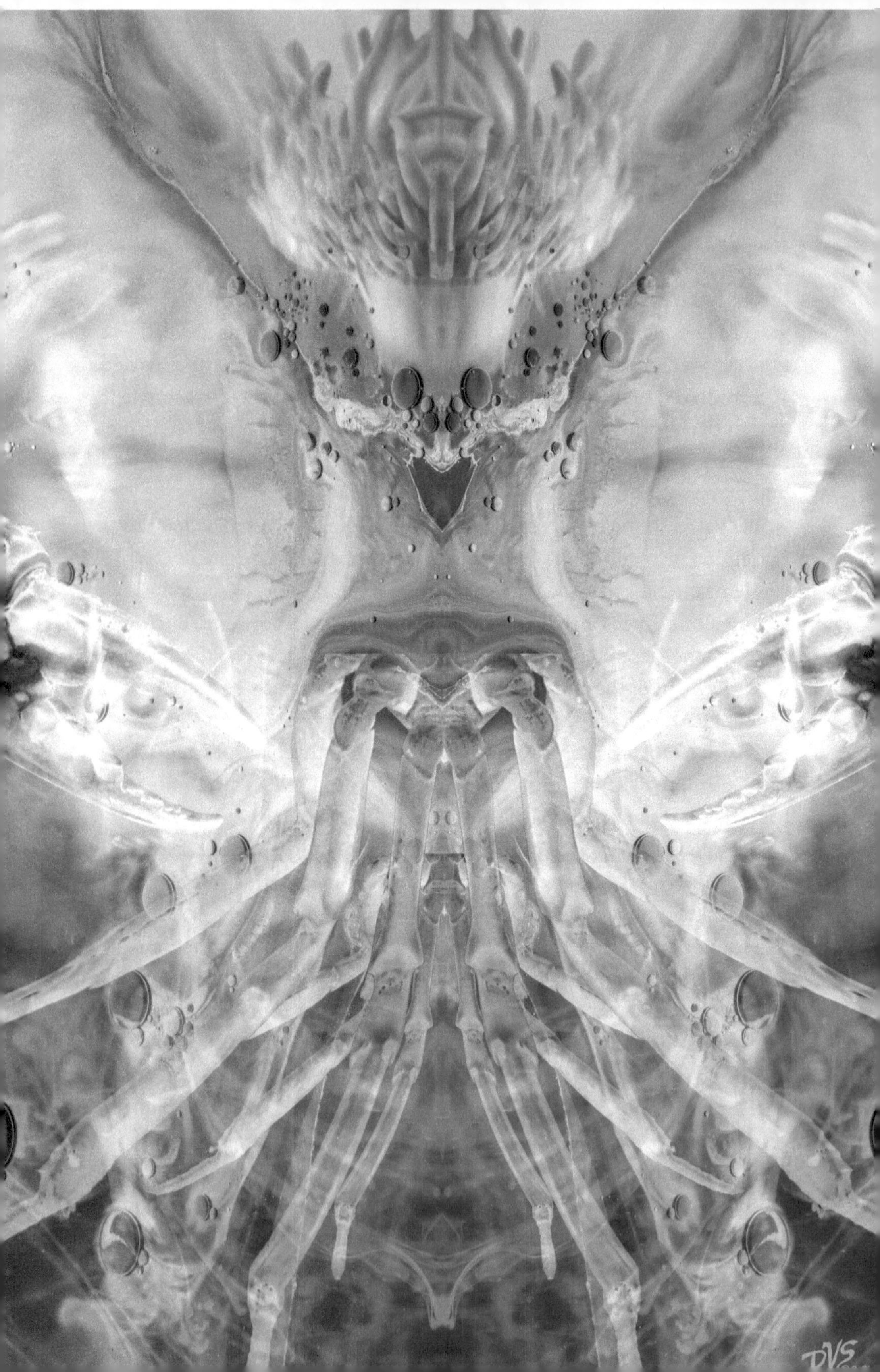

at her and smiled. The first rays of dawn were breaking over the ocean behind her. "So, that was quite a big hero move there, Mister Peaslee. Looks like you saved us all."

I feigned modesty. "You would have done the same thing."

She put one hand on the back of my head and pulled me down to her level. I thought she was going to kiss me but instead she patted me softly on the cheek. "Nope, I would have done it better, and certainly with less mess." She gestured with an arm and had me take in the disaster area that was the main hall. "What exactly are we going to tell Mr. Dudley?"

I looked at her with a touch of incredulity. "That's your concern? What we're going to tell the caretaker?"

"He's going to be here soon. I think we should get our story straight."

"We could just tell him the truth," suggested Richard Cross.

Socrates Zorba shook his head. "I would rather not have to explain certain details."

"I suspect none of you would." Megan laughed out loud. "I am going to assume that our invoice for this little adventure will be paid in full, and that you will make it clear that we had nothing to do with any of the damages."

"Of course," replied the elder Zorba. "And the two of you will be just as discrete?"

Megan smiled slyly and walked me toward the control panel. I knew what she wanted: the resonator. She wanted to destroy it, to make sure that nothing like this could ever happen again. But the resonator was gone—someone had beaten us to it.

"Do we make a fuss?" I asked in a whisper.

"Who exactly do we accuse? And on what authority do we have a claim?"

"So, who do you think has it?"

She shook her head. "Not a clue, but I know one thing."

"What's that?"

"We will find out someday. Sooner or later somebody is going to try and use it again. I just hope we aren't around to have to deal with it."

I kissed her on the cheek. "New Year's Day is just around the corner."

She tapped her left holster. "Bring it on."

ABOUT THE AUTHOR

PETER RAWLIK is a writer and book collector living in Florida. In 2000, his research for a history of the Miskatonic River Valley laid the groundwork for what would eventually become the *Reanimators* (2013), *The Weird Company* (2014), *Reanimatrix* (2016), and *The Peaslee Papers* (2017). He edited *Legacy of the Reanimator* (2015, with Brian Sammons), and *The Chromatic Court* (2019), his short story collection, *The Strange Company and Others*, was released the same year. He is a regular member of the *Lovecraft eZine* Podcast and a frequent contributor to the New York Review of Science Fiction.

ABOUT THE ARTIST

DAN SAUER is a graphic designer and artist living in Oregon. In 2016, he co-founded (with editor/publisher Obadiah Baird) *The Audient Void: A Journal of Weird Fiction and Dark Fantasy*, which features his design and illustration work. Since 2017, he has worked extensively on book covers and interior art for Hippocampus Press and other publishers. His art often takes the form of surreal collage and photomontage, as pioneered by artists such as Max Ernst, Wilfried Sätty, J. K. Potter and Harry O. Morris.

GOT WEIRD?
DON'T FORGET YOUR SHOGGOTH

From horror / sci-fi / cyberpunk legend JOHN SHIRLEY, author of *Demons*, *Wetbones* and *Lovecraft Alive!*—a unique collection of stories, organized into four sections. The first section is *Really Weird Stories*. The second is *Really, Really Weird Stories*. The third is *Really, Really, Really Weird Stories*. The fourth is—oh yes—*Really, Really, Really, Really Weird Stories*. Each section is weirder than the last, doubling its strangeness a section at a time. The collection starts out disquieting; it becomes disturbing, then it gets outrageously weird—then *mind-bending*.

The updated edition of *RRRRWS* is one of the most impressive feats of sustained and varied weirdness since Harlan Ellison's landmark *Dangerous Visions* anthologies. This edition contains four new stories, including the Lovecraftian Antarctic adventure "A Boy and His Shoggoth," and, published here for the first time, "The Whisperer Made Visible"—a tale of secret treaties with horrors eldritch and invisible.

> "A landmark collection from one of speculative fiction's wildest and greatest talents. What a joy to see it back in print!"
> —PETER ATKINS, writer of *Hellraiser 2-4* & *Wishmaster*

AVAILABLE NOW FROM

www.JackanapesPress.com
www.facebook.com/Jackanapes-Press